SAFE HARBOR

LANTERN BEACH BLACKOUT, BOOK 2

CHRISTY BARRITT

Squeaky Clean Mysteries:

#1 Hazardous Duty

#2 Suspicious Minds

#2.5 It Came Upon a Midnight Crime (novella)

#3 Organized Grime

#4 Dirty Deeds

#5 The Scum of All Fears

#6 To Love, Honor and Perish

#7 Mucky Streak

#8 Foul Play

#9 Broom & Gloom

#10 Dust and Obey

#11 Thrill Squeaker

#11.5 Swept Away (novella)

#12 Cunning Attractions

#13 Cold Case: Clean Getaway

#14 Cold Case: Clean Sweep

#15 Cold Case: Clean Break

#16 Cleans to an End (coming soon)

While You Were Sweeping, A Riley Thomas Spinoff

The Sierra Files:

#1 Pounced

#2 Hunted

#3 Pranced

#4 Rattled

The Gabby St. Claire Diaries (a Tween Mystery series):

The Curtain Call Caper

The Disappearing Dog Dilemma

The Bungled Bike Burglaries

The Worst Detective Ever

#1 Ready to Fumble

#2 Reign of Error

#3 Safety in Blunders

#4 Join the Flub

#5 Blooper Freak

#6 Flaw Abiding Citizen

#7 Gaffe Out Loud

#8 Joke and Dagger

#9 Wreck the Halls

#10 Glitch and Famous (coming soon)

Raven Remington

Relentless 1

Relentless 2 (coming soon)

Holly Anna Paladin Mysteries:

#1 Random Acts of Murder

#2 Random Acts of Deceit

#2.5 Random Acts of Scrooge

#3 Random Acts of Malice

#4 Random Acts of Greed

#5 Random Acts of Fraud

#6 Random Acts of Outrage

#7 Random Acts of Iniquity

Lantern Beach Mysteries

#1 Hidden Currents

#2 Flood Watch

#3 Storm Surge

#4 Dangerous Waters

#5 Perilous Riptide

#6 Deadly Undertow

Lantern Beach Romantic Suspense

Tides of Deception

Shadow of Intrigue

Storm of Doubt

Winds of Danger

Lantern Beach P.D.

On the Lookout

Attempt to Locate

First Degree Murder

Dead on Arrival

Plan of Action

Lantern Beach Escape

Afterglow (a novelette)

Lantern Beach Blackout

Dark Water

Safe Harbor

Ripple Effect

Carolina Moon Series

Home Before Dark

Gone By Dark

Wait Until Dark

Light the Dark

Taken By Dark

Suburban Sleuth Mysteries:
Death of the Couch Potato's Wife

Fog Lake Suspense:
Edge of Peril
Margin of Error
Brink of Danger
Line of Duty

Cape Thomas Series:
Dubiosity
Disillusioned
Distorted

Standalone Romantic Mystery:
The Good Girl

Suspense:
Imperfect
The Wrecking

Sweet Christmas Novella:
Home to Chestnut Grove

Standalone Romantic-Suspense:

Keeping Guard

The Last Target

Race Against Time

Ricochet

Key Witness

Lifeline

High-Stakes Holiday Reunion

Desperate Measures

Hidden Agenda

Mountain Hideaway

Dark Harbor

Shadow of Suspicion

The Baby Assignment

The Cradle Conspiracy

Trained to Defend

Nonfiction:

Characters in the Kitchen

Changed: True Stories of Finding God through Christian Music (out of print)

The Novel in Me: The Beginner's Guide to Writing and Publishing a Novel (out of print)

CHAPTER ONE

"DON'T you know you're killing me? Bringing me so much misery? It's like I'm dying slowly with every breath I take. It's a prison for me that you've worked so hard to create. You're killing me."

People around Bree Jordan screamed as bright lights shone down into her eyes, nearly blinding her. The bass guitar reverberated, every beat matching the rhythm of her heart. Behind her, a huge screen showed images of crime-scene tape. Of flashing police lights. Of a brooding, handsome man standing in the shadows.

Dramatics.

Bree's producer knew how to put on a show. There was no doubt about that.

Yet, as she stood in front of the audience, only one thought echoed in her mind. *Is this all there is?*

Wealth, fame, and beauty were supposed to be the pinnacle of success. If that was true, why did Bree feel so empty right now?

As the song ended, a chilly breeze swept around her, pushing her hair from her face. She couldn't have asked for better timing. It was almost like a wind machine had been turned on, adding to the drama of the moment.

It may have been fifty degrees outside, but the breeze coming off the water had more bite to it than a shark at feeding time.

That hadn't stopped the crowds from coming. Last Bree had heard, six thousand tickets had been sold. She was wrapping up her role as headliner for the first annual Lantern Beach Music Festival.

"Bree . . . Bree . . . Bree," the crowd chanted.

She swallowed hard as she tried to see beyond the bright lights to the crowd.

Was he here? Her stalker?

He seemed to be wherever Bree went. Always there. Always watching.

"You okay?" Lloyd Marks, one of her guitarists, nudged her. She couldn't hear him, not with the in-ear monitors plugging her ears. But she'd read his lips.

Bree snapped back to the present, realizing her preoccupation had taken over. These people had paid to hear her sing. That's what she needed to do. She couldn't just stand on the stage and let fear get the best of her.

Right on schedule, her drummer, Bobby Dee, pulled out some beach balls and threw them into the audience. She could hear the screams of pleasure. She could barely see the balls bouncing in the air. But she could feel the excitement around her.

Excitement because of her.

You've got everything you ever asked for. Don't blow it, Bree. There are thousands of hopefuls who'd gladly take your place.

Bree nodded at Lloyd, letting him know she was ready to continue. Then she plastered on a smile. She needed to put on the show of her life right now and hide any hints of her inner turmoil. Her fans deserved that much, at least.

The strains of her next song began. The audience recognized the tune, and their cheers grew louder.

Bree sucked in a deep breath before belting the first lyrics. "You think you know me, but you don't.

You think I am lovely, but I'm not. You think you're awesome, and I think you're hot. So why don't we just see what we've got?"

She inwardly cringed at the lyrics. Bree had begged her manager, Emerson, not to make her record this song. But he'd insisted the catchy beat would be a hit, despite the dimwitted lyrics.

He'd been right. This song had been a smashing success. Number one on the Billboard Hot 100 for the past month. It had propelled her to new heights of fame.

I think you're hot, so why don't we just see what we've got?

Certainly, people had more depth than this? Bree didn't want to bite the hand that fed her, but she wasn't sure these lyrics were what she wanted to be known for.

Despite that, she kept singing. Kept putting on a show. Giving her fans what they wanted.

She'd left everything behind to pursue this career.

And every day Bree asked herself if the sacrifices were worth it.

The song ended, and Lloyd strummed his guitar, showboating in front of the crowds. He knew what the fans wanted. The cheers from the throngs fed him, egged him on. The man was a true entertainer.

As Bree's fans moved closer to the stage, security guards pushed them back. The bright lights still blinded her, but she could see the hands reaching toward her from the front row.

At one time, she wouldn't have feared those hands. She would have understood her fans' adoration. She'd had her favorite singers as well.

Now, she didn't know whom to trust. Everyone seemed suspect.

Bree's gaze went to a man leaning over the stage. He was blond, with harshly gelled hair and pale skin.

It wasn't his hair or skin that drew Bree's attention, however. It was the look in his eyes. Something about the man seemed off.

Or had her stalker just messed with her head?

"Bree!" The next moment, the man tried to scramble onto the stage. One of her bodyguards grabbed him, yanked the man's hands behind him, and led him away.

Bree's heart thrummed in her ears.

How did she know it was safe here?

The concert area was outside. She might as well be a bottle on a fence post.

Sweat formed on her brow. Suddenly, this show seemed like a very bad idea. What had she been thinking when she agreed?

"One last song," Lloyd mouthed to her, as if he could sense her anxiety and distraction. "You're a star, Bree. You can do this."

The band knew about the threats. Bree had no choice but to tell them after her last concert had been evacuated because of a false bomb threat. Was her stalker behind it? She didn't know for sure, but she had to assume he was.

"Anyone want to be my boyfriend?" Bree asked, keeping her voice low but perky—just like she'd been trained.

The line was rehearsed. Had been spoon-fed to her. Had been written as a lead into her next song.

She hated it.

But the crowd *loved* it. They yelled. Screamed. Threw the beach balls into the air.

Bree pulled herself together as Lloyd began the intro. "Boyfriend" was supposed to be her next hit, and it had just about as much depth as the last number she'd sung.

"I want to be your girlfriend. Do you want to be my boyfriend? Together, I think we could be something special. Yes, we're the recipe for successful."

Bree did her best to give her fans exactly what they wanted in a show. They wanted to be entertained. To feel like they knew her. To feel like they were living out songs vicariously through her.

But halfway through the intrepid lyrics to "Boyfriend," a new sound filled the air.

Bree froze. That wasn't feedback from the guitar. It wasn't Bobby Dee hitting the bass drum a little too loud. Nor was it an audience member who'd brought a noisemaker.

It was—

"Get down!" Before Bree realized what was happening, someone tackled her.

One of her bodyguards.

The sound filled the air again.

It was a gunshot, she realized.

Somebody was shooting at her.

***

"WE'VE GOT to get you out of here." Dez Rodriquez hovered over Bree, determined not to let his emotions get the best of him. He'd had plenty of practice on the battlefield. A clear head and sound logic were the key to survival right now.

However, the beachfront concert was supposed

to represent the American dream, not the war-ravaged countries he'd fought in.

He'd been hired to do one thing: protect popstar Bree Jordan during her concert. Had anyone imagined it was going to turn into this? How could they?

Using his body as a shield, Dez moved beside Bree. Thank goodness he'd worn a bulletproof vest. If he died in the line of duty, he'd imagined it happening while at war or while overthrowing a corrupt government or taking down a dictator. Not while guarding a pop princess.

More gunfire came from the direction of the ocean.

The audience ran. Scattered. Panic filled the air. More people onstage ran, yelled.

His colleagues would handle the pandemonium in the audience. He needed to concentrate on Bree, despite the fact that she looked like the woman who broke his heart. Every time he saw her, bad memories filled him.

Dez shoved the thought aside and kept moving, kept hovering, kept guarding her life with his own.

Before he reached the edge of the stage, something sliced his shoulder.

He grunted.

A bullet had grazed him.

He glanced at Bree. She appeared to be okay.

That was all that mattered right now.

Finally, they reached the oversized speakers at the corner of the platform. An officer there helped Bree down the steps. Dez followed behind, keeping an arm around her.

He had to get her out of sight.

Remaining low, they reached the backstage area. It wasn't secure back here. The large screens that had been set up would offer little protection—only a false sense of security. As he glanced up, he saw the holes the bullets had cut through the material.

Dez kept moving until they were behind a vehicle that had been left backstage.

Bree would be safe.

For now.

CHAPTER TWO

AS MORE GUNFIRE RANG OUT, Bree squeezed her eyes shut. She wanted this to be a nightmare. But it wasn't.

People were hurt.

And it was her fault.

"Are you okay?" Her bodyguard kneeled in front of her, his brown eyes searching hers.

She nodded, but her head spun. "I . . . I think."

"Stay here."

She nodded, but, as the man started to rise to his feet, she grabbed his arm. "Don't leave me."

His gaze softened. "I won't. I'm just seeing what's going on."

Bree's eyes sank, and she sucked in a breath when she saw his shoulder. "You're bleeding."

He glanced down and shrugged. "The bullet just grazed my arm. It could've been much worse. I'll worry about that in a minute. We're going to make sure nothing happens to you first."

But the world felt like it was falling apart around her, and she was powerless to do anything to stop it. A cry escaped her lips.

In the background, she heard one of her songs blare through the speakers.

You're killing me.

Somehow, a recording played.

The song was supposed to be used for the encore. Bree was going to step out and the recording would fade as live music took over.

Fans had loved it at her other concerts.

Now it seemed like a sad testament to a shallow career—one that would end in tragedy.

The lyrics rang out. "I'm dying. I'm dying. I'm dying because of you."

Bree's muscles turned to gelatin at the irony.

DEZ IGNORED the pain that ripped through his shoulder. He had to concentrate on keeping Bree safe.

He thought this assignment would be easy. Mostly, it involved keeping this woman's adoring fans away from her.

No one had anticipated this.

Memories of the battlefield continued to haunt him. Especially that last black ops mission he'd been a part of. The one where his leader, Daniel Oliver, had died.

Only moments before a bullet had taken his life, Daniel had rushed past Dez and whispered a secret. A secret that no one except Dez knew—not even the other members of his SEAL platoon.

This is only the tip of the iceberg. Be careful who you trust.

The words still haunted Dez to this day.

Other band members scrambled behind the stage. Shock was evident on their features. In their wide eyes. Their quick motions. Their parted lips.

Bree squeezed his arm again—she hadn't let go. "The shooter . . . did he get anyone else?"

Dez glanced around and spotted a man being carried away from the stage by two of the event staff. Blood stained the man's shirt, and his eyes were closed as his face scrunched with pain. Staff members lowered him to the ground to examine him until the EMTs arrived.

Bree followed his gaze and let out a gasp. She darted away from Dez and toward the injured man. "Lloyd! Oh, Lloyd!"

Dez glanced around one more time, looking for any trouble.

He saw nothing, and Bree was low enough that the stage should protect her.

The wounded man—Lloyd, Bree had called him—moaned as he lay on the ground. The two staffers knelt by him as the man grasped his midsection. Blood stained his shirt.

"Oh, Lloyd . . ." Bree said again, kneeling beside him.

It didn't look good. The man was losing a lot of blood.

A paramedic who'd been on standby rushed toward Lloyd. Sirens sounded in the distance.

"Dez, are you okay?" a new voice asked.

He looked up to see his boss, Colton Locke, dart toward him. Urgency strained each of his motions. This was a full-blown emergency.

Dez glanced at his shoulder, at the patch of blood there, and nodded. "I'll be fine. Just a surface wound."

"And Bree?"

Dez glanced at the woman again and nodded. "She's scared but not hurt."

"Keep an eye on things back here. I'm going to see if Chief Chambers needs any help. It's a madhouse out there."

Dez nodded. He could still hear the crowd. People were still screaming, crying, darting away in fear.

What a disaster.

Dez hoped they caught whoever was behind this. No one should get away with an act like this. No one.

CHAPTER THREE

BREE SAT in the chapel of the Lantern Beach Medical Clinic and ran a tissue beneath her eyes. Her face felt raw from wiping it so much, but she couldn't stop.

Lloyd was in surgery right now. If treatment hadn't been so urgent, he would've probably been transported to a bigger hospital. But since time was of the essence, the Lantern Beach doctor had been forced to operate on him because of internal bleeding.

Besides her bodyguard, three other people at the concert had also been shot, but their injuries appeared to be non-life threatening. They were also being treated.

She was thankful for that. It could have been so much worse.

The guys from her band were in the chapel with her. They'd caused too much of a commotion in the waiting room. Fans had been clamoring for autographs. This clinic had turned into a circus. Bree doubted the small Lantern Beach police force had enough staff to manage the scene from the concert as well as the craziness here at the clinic.

The fanfare was unnecessary at a time like this. Families still needed time to process what had happened.

Bree glanced over her shoulder and saw that her bodyguard still stood beside her. Apparently, the man couldn't leave her side until this was all over, and Bree wasn't going to argue. Having the imposing man close made her feel safe.

He'd already been stitched up, had a bandage peeking out from under his sleeve, and someone had brought him a fresh T-shirt—absent of the blood stains and bullet hole. Based on his stiff demeanor, no one would have guessed he'd just been shot. Instead, he was all focus and determination.

Her manager, Emerson Platt, strode into the room and sat beside her. The man was short and scrawny. His motions—and words—were always fast. It felt like a whirlwind whenever he came around.

Emerson paused, a cup of coffee in his hand. He looked more like he'd just come from a meeting than a tragedy. How did he keep such a cool head?

Bree wasn't impressed—more like bothered.

"How are you?" he asked.

"I should've never done this concert," Bree mumbled. It was the only thing she could think about. Emerson had told her to say no when she'd been invited.

The crowd here at the festival was much smaller than her sold-out arenas. The pay wasn't as good. Her band had been pared down.

But, for some reason, she'd felt compelled to say yes. This place reminded her of her roots, her beginnings. She'd wanted to give back.

Big mistake.

"You couldn't have known." Emerson leaned into the wooden pew, causing the whole thing to groan.

"No, but maybe we should have anticipated something like this happening. This is all my fault." Bree's head pounded as she said the words.

"Don't be ridiculous, Bree. No one will blame you."

"I don't know how they can't." This was her show.

People had trusted that the event would be secure. Emerson didn't seem to understand that, though. He was always so focused, so absent of emotion—at least, emotions like compassion and empathy.

Emerson let out a long breath and shifted. "How long are you going to stay?"

"Until Lloyd is out of surgery." Bree had already made up her mind, and no one would talk her out of it.

"We don't know how long that will be."

"It doesn't matter how long it will be. I'm staying."

He raised his eyebrows. "Okay then. Have it your way. You just look like you could use some rest."

"I'll be fine." Bree's words contained a harder edge than she'd intended, but Emerson had always annoyed her. If he wasn't so good at what he did, she would have fired him a long time ago. But he was the one who'd made her a star, a fact he reminded her of as often as possible.

"I'm going to continue to do damage control." Emerson stood. "I have some phone calls I need to make, but I'll check in later."

Once Emerson started toward the door, Bree almost felt better. He wasn't the type to calm her down. No, he was the type who stirred up her insecurities and fears.

Bree closed her eyes. Flashbacks of the gunfire hit her. She flinched with every memory.

None of this seemed real. How could this happen at her concert?

Even worse, had anyone told Jill yet? Jill was Lloyd's longtime girlfriend. She couldn't find out about something like this on the news.

"Emerson!" she called.

He paused at the door.

"Have you talked to Jill?" she asked.

"Not yet."

"Let me. She needs to hear it from me."

He stared at her for a moment before nodding. "Very well."

Bree picked up her phone. It had been left in the car she'd taken to the concert. Emerson had retrieved it for her earlier.

Nausea churned in her stomach as she stared at the screen. This was the last thing she wanted to do. But it was the right thing, so she had no other choice.

DEZ LISTENED to the conversation behind him. For this role, he was paid to be faceless but present. To be invisible yet out in front. To be close but like a ghost.

He'd worked jobs like this plenty of times before. But, right now, he was having trouble keeping his distance and remaining purely professional.

Bree Jordan's manager seemed like a real jerk. Maybe the man was just doing his job. Maybe he was paid the big bucks to do image control and to care about things that seemed trivial. But, in a situation like this, the man just seemed insensitive.

Dez listened as Bree talked on the phone to a woman—Lloyd's girlfriend, Jill, from what Dez understood. Compassion squeezed in his chest.

Just listening to it brought back memories of the day Dez had gone with their friend Colton to tell Daniel's wife, Elise, that her husband had died during a covert operation. A lump formed in his throat at the memory.

As Bree ended the call, he heard her sniffle behind him.

Whenever Dez had seen Bree on TV, she'd always looked so happy and perky, like she didn't have a care in the world. But right now the weight of that very world hung on her shoulders.

Red blotches marred her pretty face. She needed to have someone here for her. But the one person that Dez had expected would step up—her manager—had left to make some phone calls.

The rest of the band—three other members—were here. Each of them seemed stoic, though, and almost in shock. They were being called one by one to give their statement to the police.

Dez was anxious to hear an update on the situation from Colton. He wanted to know if this guy had been caught. But, right now, he just needed to concentrate on keeping Bree safe.

"You can sit down if you want, you know," a soft voice said.

Dez quickly glanced behind him and saw that Bree was talking to him. Her voice had sounded much gentler than he'd expected.

Bree, with her platinum blonde hair that flowed in perfect waves down to her shoulders. With her ripped black jeans, bright red shirt, and knee-high boots. Her eye makeup was dark and heavy. Her lips matched her shirt. Only now, everything appeared smeared since she'd been crying and wiping her eyes.

She looked like . . . a star. A beautiful, tortured star.

"I'm okay standing," he finally told her.

"It's been hours, though. You have to be tired."

"This is what I do. Don't worry about me." He remained in front of her, just in case trouble showed up. Two of his colleagues were in the waiting room area, trying to control the people there.

"What's your name?" Bree's voice came out sounding squeaky. She seemed to notice and rubbed her throat.

He glanced at her again. "Dez. Dez Rodriguez."

"Nice to meet you, Mr. Rodriquez."

"Just Dez is fine."

"Dez, then. And you can just call me Bree." She paused. "You took a bullet for me."

"It's my job."

"I don't know how you do your job then. I would never be that courageous."

"It's not that bad. Besides, this scar will give me something else to talk about."

"That's one way to look at it." Her voice softened. "I suppose scars are great storytellers. You know what? That kind of sounds like a song."

"You should write it then." Maybe this conversation would help distract her for a moment from her burdens.

Bree let out an airy chuckle. "They won't ever let me use the songs I write."

He quickly glanced at her again, her words surprising him. "Really? I assumed you wrote all the songs that you sang."

She practically snorted. "No, they won't let me. They weren't looking for a singer and songwriter. They were looking for a popstar. Big difference."

Dez wasn't sure what that meant. He didn't know how the music industry worked, and he'd never really cared to know, to be honest. But Bree sounded so sorrowful that he almost wanted to know more.

Before he could ask anything else, Doc Clemson stepped into the room. Dez braced himself to hear how Lloyd was doing. He prayed for good news.

Because he wasn't sure Bree could handle any more trauma.

BREE STOOD and held her breath, unsure what the doctor would say. But she prayed Lloyd was okay. She'd prayed hard, harder than she had prayed in years.

"How is he?" Her voice cracked.

The rest of the band crowded around also, each anxious to hear an update.

"He's going to be just fine," the doctor announced.

Bree's knees seemed to go weak. Dez caught her elbow and lowered her into the pew behind her.

"I'm so glad to hear that," she said. "I've been worried."

"Recovery will take time, but the prognosis is good. He's still groggy from the surgery, so he can't see anyone right now. But I knew you'd want to know how he was doing."

"Thank you so much," Bree rushed. "Thank you for taking good care of him in there."

Doc Clemson nodded at her, then looked at her guard and nodded at him as well.

"Would you like to stay?" Dez asked Bree.

"I would." Her gaze wandered to the crowd in the distance. "But I fear that I'm causing a circus around here. Do you think the staff could call me when Lloyd is able to have visitors? He's not close to his family, and Jill won't be here until tomorrow."

"I'm sure they can arrange something."

"Maybe it would be best for everyone if I got out of here sooner rather than later. I know people are trying to get into the waiting room, just so they can see me. I want this time to be focused on the victims and not on me."

Just as the words left her mouth, a man darted into the chapel.

It was the same man who'd tried to get on the stage earlier, Bree realized. The one whose eyes looked crazy.

She felt the breath leave her lungs. Had he been the same one who'd pulled the trigger earlier today?

As the man yelled her name, Bree braced herself for the worst.

CHAPTER FOUR

DEZ STEPPED in front of Bree, ready to stop this lunatic in his tracks.

The man's eyes were wide and his pupils dilated. His skin was covered with sweat. His breath was shallow and uneven.

"Bree!" The man lunged toward her, desperation in his eyes.

Dez raised his hand and pushed the man back. "That's far enough, buddy."

"I'm your biggest fan!" He clawed at Dez's chest, trying to get around him. The man was small but scrappy.

"I said back off," Dez growled.

"I've loved you ever since I heard your first song."

The man craned his neck around Dez's chest, almost like he couldn't hear him.

Dez radioed one of his colleagues, Griff McIntyre, who was here at the clinic. He could use some backup right now.

"God told me that we're supposed to get married, Bree," the man said. "I know you'll see it too. You just need a little more time."

Bree let out a cry behind him.

Just then, Griff strode into the room and grabbed the man, jerking his arms behind him. "I thought you were locked up."

"They didn't have anything to hold me." The man strained to get away from Griff. "I didn't do anything wrong. I just want to see Bree."

"She doesn't want to see you," Dez said. "Now get out of here."

Griff led the man away. As he did, Dez turned back to Bree. The woman was a trembling mess—as anyone would be in her circumstance.

"I'd like to go." Her hand clutched at her neck.

"I think the police chief needs to take a statement from you. Last I heard, she's here at the clinic talking to various witnesses."

"That's fine. But I want to get out of here as soon as I can."

Dez didn't blame her for wanting to leave.

Keeping a hand on her arm, Dez glanced around again. It looked like this easy assignment was going to be anything but.

BREE FELT DAZED as Dez led her toward an office at the clinic. She didn't know this man, yet she was entirely grateful for him. Her head was spinning, and any logic had flown out the window.

Dez's gaze seemed to take in everything around them for any signs of trouble.

With a slight nod, he ushered her across the hall. No one seemed to spot her.

She took a few deep breaths. Tragedy on top of scrutiny and grief weren't a good combination.

Dez knocked at a door before sticking his head inside and muttering a few things to someone there. A moment later, he turned back to Bree. "The chief just needs a few more minutes. Will you be okay waiting here?"

"Hopefully," she murmured.

She studied her bodyguard a moment and ran her gaze along the sculpted muscles of his arm as he leaned against the wall. The tattoos told stories. If she knew the man better, she might ask what they meant. It might be a good distraction.

Either way, this man had her curious.

"How long have you been doing this, Dez?" she asked.

"I was a Navy SEAL for twelve years. I've been doing this type of work for a few months."

"A Navy SEAL?" She crossed her arms and leaned against the wall. "You guys are all the rage right now."

"Don't believe everything you see in Hollywood."

"Only if you don't believe everything you read in the tabloids about me."

"It's a deal." He glanced at her, his eyes sparkling.

She smiled. She already liked this guy—more than she did her usual bodyguards, at least. This one had some personality.

Since her normal entourage wasn't with her today, she could use some strong people around her. Normally, her assistant was a great sounding board, but Bree had given her some time off. Bree had even told her hair and makeup artists that they could stay home.

Bree frowned as she realized what that meant. She was all alone here. Staying in a house by herself.

It wasn't ideal. Not by any means.

Bree hoped that word didn't leak about where she was staying tonight. People did the craziest things when they knew. Tried to break in to get her autograph. Camped outside in the yard. Took selfies they posted online with her house in the background. Privacy was a thing of the past.

Fame was nothing like Bree had imagined it to be. It was like standing on a platform while people simultaneously threw flowers and rotten eggs at you. It was both beautiful and tragic. A thrill and a disappointment. Could one ever truly be prepared for the dichotomy?

A few minutes later, Dez and Bree were ushered in to see the chief.

"Chief Cassidy Chambers." The woman in uniform behind the desk extended her hand.

"Bree Jordan."

"I'll leave you two to talk." Dez pointed to the door behind him.

"No. Stay. Please." Bree needed someone else to listen to her story. To fill in the gaps. To know what was going on.

"If that's what you want." Dez closed the door and then sat in the chair beside her, across from the doc's desk. "And if it's okay with Cassidy—Chief Chambers, I mean."

"That's fine with me."

Bree glanced at the police chief in front of her. The woman didn't look anything like she'd expected. Not that Bree knew exactly what to expect, but certainly not a pretty blonde who looked only a few years older than she was.

Bree was kind of impressed. She loved seeing women in positions of power that were normally held by men.

"I'm sorry about everything that happened today." The chief frowned and leaned against the desk. Lines of exhaustion seemed to be etched on her forehead. No doubt her day had been just as crazy as Bree's. "We're trying to figure out what's going on."

"I'm sorry that I brought all of this chaos to your island. Please tell me you caught the person responsible."

Chief Chambers' frown deepened. "I wish we could say that we had. He was on a boat. He pulled near the shore with a semi-automatic, pulled the trigger, and hit anything—and anybody—that was in the way."

Bree sucked in a shallow breath at the stark reminder of what had happened. "So he's still out there?"

The police chief nodded, her gaze somber. "I wish I could tell you something different, but he hasn't been caught yet. I assure you that every law enforcement agency in this area is looking for him now. The Coast Guard has boats scouring the water at this very moment as well as the marine police."

"How could he have gotten away?" It just seemed too unfathomable. Bree's only comfort was in thinking that this guy had finally been caught. But she couldn't even rest easier with that thought now.

"I don't think anybody was anticipating having trouble from the water."

"No, I don't suppose that they would. What can I do to help you catch him?" People had been hurt because of Bree. She had to do whatever possible to help put this guy behind bars. She would dip into her own paycheck, if that's what it came down to.

The chief picked up a pad of paper in front of her. "Is there anybody you can think of who might have wanted to do this?"

Bree stared at the police chief, surprised she hadn't brought up the obvious. "My stalker."

The police chief just stared back at her with no sign of recognition on her expression. "Your stalker?"

Why did she look so confused? "I thought my manager told you."

"Your manager didn't tell me anything." Chief Chambers continued to study Bree, an uncertain expression on her face as she waited for Bree to explain.

Bree shook her head and squeezed the skin between her eyes. Why hadn't the police been informed?

"I've had a stalker for the last three months," she started. "His threats keep increasing. I thought my manager was going to tell you about this. He probably didn't want to pay for the extra security." Did Emerson really care about the bottom line more than he cared about people's safety?

Bree wanted to say the question was ridiculous. But was it? The fact Bree had to question it said a lot.

"The festival did hire security," the chief said.

Bree crossed her arms. "But I wanted more than what we typically have at a concert. It's what Emerson and I discussed before I came here. Outdoor concerts have challenges . . . and I'm not just talking about sound quality."

"Tell us about this stalker." Dez's gaze looked hard, inquisitive—and there was no sign of apology for inserting himself into this conversation.

Bree let out a long breath, a mental film reel of memories—bad memories—playing in her head. "He began sending me emails about three months ago. The threats have gradually escalated."

"Anything else?"

Bree glanced at her hands on her lap as she realized the truth in her words. "I feel like what happened today was all my fault."

"We're not saying that," the chief said. "The only person responsible is the person who pulled the trigger. But we do wish we had been informed of these threats before the concert today."

"Believe me, I wish you had been informed too. I'm not sure where the breakdown in communication happened, but I will be talking to my manager about this."

"Do you have any idea who the stalker is?" Chief Chambers leaned back, but the intensity in her eyes remained.

"He's been relatively faceless. He's mostly approached me on social media. At times, I thought I saw a shadow in the crowds. But, no, I've never seen his face—that I know, at least."

"Are any law enforcement agencies working on this?" Dez asked.

"Not really. I mean, I can't even file a restraining

order because I don't know this guy's name. Plus, this is a matter for local police, and I'm on the road so much that there's not one agency who can work this case."

"How long do you plan on staying here in town?" Chief Chambers asked.

"At least until Lloyd is released from the clinic."

"Did Doc Clemson say how long Lloyd might be kept at the clinic?" The chief's gaze went to Dez.

"He doesn't know, but I would say at least a couple of days with that kind of injury," Dez said.

"You don't have any other concerts to get to right now?" the chief asked.

"This was supposed to be the last concert of the tour. I'm supposed to be on a two-month break until my summer tour starts."

"I can assure you that while you are in town, we will be working this case," the chief said. "We also may have more questions for you."

"I'll be happy to answer whatever I can. I want to catch this guy. Whoever did this to Lloyd and the other concert-goers needs to be behind bars."

"I agree. I'll station an officer outside your place tonight to keep an eye on things, okay? Just to be safe."

"Yes." Bree stood. "Thank you so much for your help."

As Bree stepped from the clinic, a new wave of anxiety rushed over her. She had no idea what would be waiting for her once she got back to her house. She didn't like the thought of that.

CHAPTER FIVE

DEZ FELT his jaw tighten as he headed down the road again.

Why hadn't Emerson told Cassidy about Bree's stalker? Security could've been handled so much differently if they had known the potential of an imminent threat. It was just irresponsible.

He didn't hold Bree accountable for it. She had made it clear that her manager was supposed to be the one handling the issue. Dez had no doubt that was true. Most popstars didn't attend to details like that themselves but had people who did it for them.

Bree was silent beside him as they headed down the road. He could only imagine what she was thinking. A tragedy like what had happened today would shake anyone up.

Not only that, but the event was sure to be all over the news already. Dez had no doubt that camera crews were playing footage of what had happened. Bree's name would be all over the headlines. This couldn't be the kind of publicity she either wanted or needed.

He pulled up to the house where she was staying. It was one of the McMansions on the beach. The place probably had ten bedrooms, as well as an entertainment room, game room, and multiple other luxuries.

He parked in the driveway and paused. He would walk Bree inside and check out the place to make sure it was safe. He didn't want to take any chances, especially after everything that had happened.

Cassidy's officer should be arriving any time, and then the police could take over. Dez's job was done, even though part of him wanted to stay. Still, he couldn't impose. It wouldn't be professional.

He climbed out of the car and ran around to get her. As he did, his gaze swept the area once more. He saw nothing.

Except...

Was that a person moving in the brush next door?

He gripped Bree's arm. "Get back into the car, stay low, and lock the doors."

"What's going on?" Fear quivered in her voice, and her wide eyes stared back up at him.

"I don't know for sure, but there's something I'm going to check out."

She did as he asked.

When Dez knew Bree was safe, he withdrew his gun and crept toward the foliage.

Darkness had fallen hours ago. A single light was on at the house next door, but he saw no other movement. A line of brush—sea grass, a few small cedars, and clumps of thorny vines—separated the properties.

It had almost looked like someone was hiding out there.

It could be a crazy fan, he reminded himself. Just because someone lingered on the property didn't mean that person was the shooter. Dez needed to be careful.

"Who's out there?" he called. "This is private property, and you're trespassing."

He continued to pace forward as he waited for a response.

There was none.

What was this person hiding? Had they run?

Dez needed to find out.

As he stepped into the brush, his muscles tensed. Nobody was there. But Dez was certain he'd seen someone. Where could this person have gone?

Dez needed to get back to Bree. Now.

As he turned, a bullet pierced the air.

Glass shattered.

Dez's heart pounded in his chest.

Bree. He prayed that Bree was okay.

BREE HEARD THE GUNSHOT.

She had been about to sink lower into her seat when the windshield shattered. Shards of glass rained down on her, and a cool wind swept inside.

The frigid breeze reminded her that nowhere was safe. That there was nowhere she was invisible. That being untouchable was a fallacy.

Fear hammered in her chest, pounded in her ears, rose with her blood pressure.

The shooter. He was here. He had found her.

What should she do next?

Was he coming for her now? Would he grab her before Dez could get back?

Or what if he shot Dez . . . ?

She squeezed her eyes shut but only for a moment.

Please, God . . .

There she went again. Praying again. It came back so naturally to her in her times of need. It made her feel like a friend who only showed up when she needed something—and that realization made her dislike herself.

Bree waited, expecting to hear another bullet.

Instead, she heard tires squealing away.

Dez appeared, gun in hand, running to the car. He leaned on her window and yelled, "Are you okay?"

She nodded, even though she felt anything but okay. But Bree knew her injuries weren't the kind that anyone could see. They were the kind that crawled around inside her, hiding just out of sight. Sometimes, those were the worst kind. It was too easy to hide the gaping wounds even as they festered.

Dez pulled out his phone and muttered something into the device. Still glancing around, he tapped on her window. She quickly unlocked the car door, and he opened it for her. Bree climbed out, trying not to step too close to the man. Yet she craved his presence. She craved safety.

Shards of glass fell from her clothing onto the ground. The sound made her muscles tighten.

Someone had tried to kill her again.

He hadn't succeeded at the concert, but he wasn't going to give up, was he?

Just because the shooter had missed yet again, Bree knew without a doubt that he would continue trying until he got what he intended.

Her head spun at the thought.

Dez's gaze continued to search everything around him as he shielded her body with his own.

She'd halfway expected Dez to go after the shooter. But the man couldn't keep her safe and chase after a criminal. She appreciated the fact that he was here with her now.

"We need to get you inside," he muttered. "Help is on the way. Are you sure you're okay?"

"Just scared."

"Come on." He kept an arm around her, and his gaze continued to sweep the area as he led her to the house.

At the entrance, Bree punched in the code. As soon as the door opened and she stepped inside, immediate relief rushed through her. She felt safe here. At least for now.

There was only one thing she knew for sure. She

needed protection with her 24/7. She wouldn't survive without it.

She looked at Dez, at his stiff muscles and tight jaw. So far, he'd proven himself to be very reliable.

"I need to hire you. I need you to keep me safe until this man is found. I'll pay you whatever you ask." She rubbed her neck, feeling the burn in her throat. "I'm not ready to die yet."

CHAPTER SIX

DEZ STOOD in the entryway to Bree's rental house and tried to gather his thoughts.

Bree stared up at him, her eyes wide with fear and an innocence that startled him. He'd expected the woman to be worldly, maybe even arrogant. Not so homegrown and authentic. But maybe the situation had brought out these traits in her. Either way, she'd taken him by surprise.

She'd just offered to extend his contract as her bodyguard.

"I need to call my boss." Dez reminded himself to go through the proper channels before promising anything. He didn't know what else Colton had planned for this week.

"Do that. I'll pay. Whatever the price." Bree didn't even flinch as she said the words.

"You don't need to talk to your manager?"

"This isn't his choice. It's my life, and this is what I have decided." Her face hardened.

Dez stared at her another moment, sensing the tension between her and her manager. Finally, he nodded. "Okay then. In the meantime, I want to check out the rest of your house and make sure it's secure."

"I'm coming with you this time. I don't want to stay here alone."

It took a considerable amount of time to check all the rooms at the house. But the place appeared to be secure. At least that was a small measure of good news after such a tragic day.

"What management company did you rent through?" Dez asked as they headed back toward the living area on the top floor.

She shrugged. "I have no idea. My manager handled that for me."

Just like he was supposed to handle security. Dez didn't know the man, but he already didn't like him.

"We need to change the key code to the house. No doubt half the people at the management company know the code, everyone from the cleaners to the maintenance staff. We don't want anyone to get any ideas."

"I am in favor of that."

"I have a security system that we can set up temporarily. My colleagues will need to give me a hand. The process is extensive. In the meantime, are you the only one staying here?"

"Yes, I am."

"Then I'll need to make sure you have the most secure room in the house. No room that has an outside entrance. The view may not be as pretty, but it will be safer."

"Whatever you need to do."

Dez stared at her again, harder this time, but then he nodded. "Okay, let's get started. We don't have any time to waste."

AN HOUR LATER, alarms had been set on all the windows at Bree's house. The police had come and taken statements, as well as photographed the shattered car windshield. Dez had talked to his team about setting up a rotation.

Bree felt a raging headache coming on. She grabbed her favorite seltzer water from the fridge and paused by the kitchen counter as Dez chatted with someone on the phone.

She got her first real look at him.

That wasn't exactly the truth. She had noticed the man right away. Who wouldn't? He was the kind of man who was easily noticed and couldn't be ignored.

His skin was light brown and his hair dark, almost black. He had muscles that could be seen for miles, and a smile that could be seen even farther.

He looked more like he could be an actor in Hollywood than a bodyguard here on this small island. And he was a former Navy SEAL? Bree wondered what his story was.

She'd had plenty of bodyguards over the past two years. Most of them didn't capture her attention the way this man did. For that matter, most of them simply did their job and stayed at a distance. Some had asked for autographs for their kids or other loved ones. But there seemed to be something different about Dez Rodriguez.

He was a nice distraction in the midst of an otherwise horrible day. Still, he was too much like the players who'd broken her heart in the past. Why was she always attracted to that type? The ones who only wanted to have fun.

Bree took a sip of her water, the events from today slamming back into her mind. Everything still felt surreal.

She couldn't believe that someone had opened fire at her concert. She couldn't believe that people were injured. Or that someone had shot at her here at the house.

Had the whole world gone crazy? That's how it felt. Then again, Bree's world had felt like it was spinning out of control for a long time now.

Insisting on having a place to stay by herself had been her first step in taking that control back, as had coming here for this concert.

Success wasn't supposed to feel like this. Yet, Bree felt like she couldn't complain. This was what she had prayed for. Who was she to always think the grass was greener on the other side?

She wanted to live with an attitude of gratitude. Her sixth-grade teacher had had a big poster in the classroom with those words on it. Despite the cheesy rhyme, the words were still true. Bree wanted to be thankful for the opportunities she'd been given instead of complaining about them. However, that slope felt slippery.

Dez ended his call and lowered his phone. She waited for what he had to say.

"Our guard rotation is all set up."

"That sounds great. I'm really sorry you're having to go through all of this trouble for me."

Dez leaned against the counter. "It's no trouble. Keeping you safe is our priority."

"It sounds like you're good at what you do."

"Whatever we're doing, we give it our best."

"That's a good motto to live by." As she took another sip of her water, her phone rang. Her eyes widened when she saw the clinic's number.

Quickly, she put the phone to her ear. It was Lloyd's doctor.

"Your friend is awake," he said. "I just wanted to let you know. Normally, we don't have visiting hours now. But he's asking for you. And, considering the circumstances, we'll bend the rules for you this one time."

"Thank you," Bree muttered. "I'll be right there."

CHAPTER SEVEN

"I'M NOT sure it's safe to leave the house." Dez had heard enough of their conversation to know what Bree was going to say next. And his priority wasn't to look after Lloyd but to keep Bree safe.

"It doesn't matter if it's safe or not. I need to go see Lloyd. He shouldn't wake up alone. He needs someone there, needs to know that somebody cares."

Dez nodded, admiring her determination. "My car is out of commission right now. But I can have one of my friends come with his car."

"If you don't mind, that would be great. Just add it to my tab."

Her words caused him to pause. How nice would it be just to be able to spend money without giving it a second thought. It was never a luxury Dez had as a SEAL—a fact that Leah, his former girlfriend, had resented.

He called Griff, who promised to be right over and give them a ride.

True to his word, Griff arrived five minutes later, and they climbed into his car. Dez sat in the backseat with Bree, keeping an eye out for any signs of danger as Griff drove.

He could sense Bree's anxiety as she sat beside him during the drive to the clinic. Anxiety in a situation like this was good. It would keep her sharp. That's what she needed right now until they knew who was behind these violent acts.

When they arrived at the clinic, they went in through a back entrance. A nurse waited there to let them in since reporters were still at the front of the building.

Dez kept one hand on Bree's arm as he led her inside. He felt her tremble. All of this had shaken her up—yet she hadn't let it stop her. He had to admire that.

This wing of the clinic had been closed off to anyone except patients and their visitors. That was a good thing. A few people paused as Bree walked in, their gazes drifting toward her. Visiting hours were over, so these were either patients or their family members.

Fame . . . it appeared it could be a blessing or a curse. Was there any such thing as privacy when you were in the spotlight all the time? It didn't appear so.

Doc Clemson met them outside Lloyd's door. He muttered a few things to Bree before ushering her inside.

"I'll wait out here for you," Dez said.

She looked up at him and nodded, a flash of gratitude in her eyes. "Thank you."

Then she disappeared inside the room.

Dez turned to Griff, sensing his friend's gaze on him.

"What?" Dez asked.

Griff shrugged in the teasing way he was known for. "Nothing."

His friend shoved his hands into his pockets, as if trying to look casual. Dez wasn't buying it.

"You're thinking something," Dez said. "Spit it out."

Griff shrugged again, a smile still playing on his lips. "She's pretty."

Realization washed over Dez. He knew what his friend was hinting at—but he was going to make Griff say it. "There are a lot of pretty girls out there."

"You do remember our policy, right? No dating clients."

Dez shrugged, making it clear Griff's words hadn't affected him. "I have no intention of making any moves on Bree Jordan."

"Good to know. But you're going to be tempted." Griff twisted his head, his gaze probing and filled with certainty.

"You think you know me so well." Dez clucked his tongue.

"I know that all the ladies like you."

"You jealous?" Dez teased.

"Jealous?" Griff chuckled. "I couldn't even handle one woman. No way do I want to try to juggle a whole mob of admirers."

"It does take a special talent." Dez flashed a smile.

Griff chuckled again. "Then that is one talent that you have mastered."

"Besides, Bree's not my type. She's too much like Leah."

Griff raised an eyebrow. "Doesn't that mean she is your type then?"

"Never again. I mean, it's uncanny how much they're alike. Leah even liked to sing, just like Bree."

"Karaoke, though, right?"

Dez shrugged. "Same difference."

"Or not . . ."

Dez's grin faded as he glanced around again. He knew reporters were still outside. Some diehard fans probably still remained there also.

This was far from being over. Until it was, he had to remain on guard.

———

BREE PAUSED beside Lloyd's bed and frowned.

Her friend looked terrible. Pale. Too thin. Too haggard.

How could things change so much in just a few hours? Lloyd had always been like her big brother. He was in his mid-thirties, with shoulder-length blond hair and sparkling eyes. He'd been in this business a long time and had taken Bree under his wing when he became a part of her band.

Seeing him like this caused her heart to ache.

"I'm so sorry, Lloyd." It was all Bree could think to say. This was her fault. It didn't matter what anyone else said.

"You had nothing to do with this." His voice sounded raspy, like it was hard to talk.

"The doctor said you're going to be okay." She avoided responding to his statement.

"That's what they told me too. I guess you'll be stuck with me for a while longer."

She smiled. "I don't know what I would do on the road without you. You're always there for me when I mess up."

"It's a big job, but someone's got to do it." He looked like he tried to smile but failed.

Bree swallowed the knot in her throat. "I called Jill. She's on her way. She should be here tomorrow."

He nodded but didn't look as happy as Bree thought he might. She knew the longtime couple had been having some problems lately.

"Did they catch the guy who did this?" Lloyd's voice sounded scratchy and thin.

Bree felt the frown pull at her lips. "No, not yet. But they're looking. I've been assured that every law enforcement agency in the area is on this right now."

"Good. The person behind this can't get away with it." He paused, his eyes searching hers. "Do they think it's the same person who's been sending you threats?"

Bree's heart pounded against her chest. "That's the assumption."

Lloyd cringed and touched his side, his eyes

narrowed with pain. "How many other people were hurt?"

"Three other people got shot, plus my bodyguard. But everyone should be okay."

"That's good. It could have been a lot worse." Lloyd's eyes began to droop.

"You're right. It could've been." Thank goodness no one had died. Bree didn't know if she could have handled that. She already felt like she'd taken multiple emotional gunshots. Any more, and she might not recover.

A nurse knocked at the door before stepping inside. "He should probably get some rest now. I'm about to give him another dose of his pain medication."

Bree nodded and took a step back, allowing the nurse some space. "I'll come back and visit you tomorrow, Lloyd."

"You just concentrate on keeping yourself safe." His eyes drooped even more.

"I will. But I have to know that you're okay also."

She stepped toward the door when Lloyd called her name. She turned back toward him. The serious look on his face caused her stomach to squeeze.

"Whoever is behind this may be closer than you think," he whispered.

Alarm swept through her. "Closer than I think? What do you mean?"

But before Lloyd could explain himself, his medication must've kicked in. His eyes closed, and he drifted off to sleep.

But the unsettled feeling remained in Bree's stomach.

CHAPTER EIGHT

DEZ FOLLOWED behind Bree as she headed away from Lloyd's room. A few people in the hallway stopped her. All had been kind, even thrilled to see her.

That was good.

Dez had feared that some of them might give her a verbal lashing or try to place all the blame on her for what had happened. No one had, though.

He watched as Bree talked to each person, impressed by her kindness. Nothing about what she was doing screamed that it was all a show. Her voice sounded sincere and warm.

There were no cameras following her moves, proving this wasn't a publicity stunt. She honestly cared about the people who had been injured.

Already, Bree Jordan had surprised him in more ways than one.

Finally, after she spoke with the last person, she met Dez in the hallway. "I'm ready to go back to the house now."

"I think some of the reporters may have discovered our back entrance. I'm going to have Griff pull the car around and clear a path for us. I just wanted to give you a warning."

She nodded. "Thank you."

He escorted her toward the door, on the phone with Griff as he did so. They paused, waiting for Griff to signal that he was ready for them.

As they stood there, Bree glanced up at him. There was a new look in her eyes, a look Dez couldn't read. He had a feeling she wanted to say something.

He pulled the phone from his ear. "Is everything okay?"

Her gaze wavered back and forth as if in deep thought, and she nibbled on her lip. "I'm not sure."

He glanced around again, wondering if she'd seen some sort of danger he hadn't. He saw nothing out of the ordinary. Just a mostly empty hallway at the clinic. "What's going on?"

"It's just that, as I was leaving Lloyd's room . . ."

Bree pulled her gaze up to meet his. "He mumbled something about keeping an eye on those who are closest to me."

Dez squinted. "What do you mean?"

"That's the thing. I don't know. The nurse had just given him some medicine. It knocked him right out so he couldn't even finish the thought."

Memories hit him. Memories of Daniel's last words to him.

Last words were significant. Life-changing. Steeped in raw truth.

So what had Lloyd meant?

"What are you thinking?" Bree stared up at him.

Dez snapped back to reality. "It almost sounds like he suspects somebody in your inner circle might have something to do with this." The words sounded surreal as they left his lips.

"I know. But what sense does that make? Why would someone close to me open fire at one of my concerts?"

"I have no idea."

She frowned. "I just wanted to let you know, in case it was significant."

"It very well could be significant," Dez said. But that didn't make his job any easier. Because the people closest to Bree would know her schedule, know how she thought, and know the best ways to get to her.

Griff called and said he was ready for them. Dez braced himself to face the reporters outside.

***

BREE FELT like she was in a daze as they rode back to her house. The darkness felt even darker right now. She glanced at her watch.

It was almost midnight.

Somehow, it felt like an entire week had passed since today's concert. What a nightmare.

Right now, Bree just wanted to get back to her place and unwind a little bit.

Ten minutes later, they pulled up to the turquoise-colored building. This time, Griff and Dez both checked all the surroundings and flanked her on each side as she walked to the door.

Once inside, her shoulders drooped with relief. Maybe a long bath and a good night's sleep would be just what she needed to think clearly.

But with that thought, a new round of guilt flooded her. Who was she to be able to relax and sleep while other people were in the clinic because of that concert?

As they stood in the entryway, her gaze went to Dez's injured shoulder. He'd made it seem like it wasn't a big deal. Did he tell the truth?

"I checked on everybody else who was injured, but I didn't check on you." Bree started to reach out but thought again and dropped her hand. "How are you really?"

He touched his shoulder and shrugged. "I'm fine. Don't worry about me."

Bree nodded, even though she knew she would continue to worry. Way back before she was a popstar, people had accused her of being a mother hen. Probably because she was the oldest of four children and she'd always liked taking care of people.

The public would find that hard to believe right now since she often traveled with an entourage who took care of all of her needs. But the entourage had not been her idea. That had been Emerson's.

"Is there anywhere around here we could order dinner?" Bree started toward the stairway that led to the third-floor living area. Griff had disappeared up that way, no doubt checking out the rest of the house again. "I'm sure you're getting hungry. So am I."

"I might be able to find you something," Dez said. "What kind of food are you thinking?"

Normally, Bree would say a salad or something healthy. But right now she just craved comfort food. "I want a burger. Fries. Oh, and, on the burger, I want cheese and bacon and mayo."

Dez smiled. "You're going all out, huh?"

"What can I say? It's been a day."

"Yes, it has."

Once they reached the top floor, Dez paced into the kitchen as Griff disappeared into the master bedroom.

When she saw Dez freeze, she knew something was wrong.

Her hand went to the wall so she could steady herself. "What is it?"

Using a napkin, Dez picked up a piece of paper from the counter. "This wasn't here when we left."

Bree moved beside him, and her eyes widened when she read the words there.

I'm not done with you yet.

The blood left her head so quickly she thought she might pass out.

Whoever her stalker was, he had been in her house.

CHAPTER NINE

AN HOUR LATER, the rest of Dez's team arrived. Security cameras were put in place, and the rest of the house was checked. Dez wasn't sure how this person had gotten inside. He called the management company and made sure they'd cleared all the previous codes from the keypad at the door. They assured him that none of those codes should work anymore.

This act proved that whoever was behind this was brazen and not intimidated. That was a bad combination.

Bree looked beside herself as she soaked in all the news.

Emerson had shown up after Bree called him.

The two of them were in the living room now, and Dez tried not to listen to their conversation, yet he couldn't help but overhear.

"We need to get you out of here." The man stood in front of Bree, his hands on his hips and his voice taking on hints of a lecture.

Bree crossed her arms. "I'm not ready to leave yet."

"It's not safe."

"Let's be honest. There's nowhere that I'm going to be safe. So I can stay here and try to put an end to this, or I can keep moving and keep having this guy follow me from place to place. I'd rather stay put. You know I don't have any concerts scheduled for the next two months."

"All the media outlets are calling. They want our statement on the matter. Want to know how you're doing."

"I assume you're handling it?"

"For now. But we need to keep our forward momentum. You're supposed to be in the studio recording some new songs."

Bree stared at Emerson, her gaze unflinching. "And I told you that I needed a little downtime first."

"You have to strike while the iron is hot. If you take a break now, you're going to regret it."

This guy was laying the pressure on thick. Bree didn't seem to have a problem standing up for herself. But Dez had a hard time not stepping into the conversation.

"How can I regret it if it refreshes me to take a step back?" Bree continued. "Going at full speed will only result in burnout."

"That's not necessarily true, Bree. You just need to learn how to kick back and take it easy a little bit more. Balance. You have to teach yourself balance. Take it from me. I've done this a time or two."

Dez wished he could knock that condescending look right off Emerson's face. But he remained at a distance, keeping his gaze fixated on the windows and doors.

"That's obviously not something that I'm good at doing," Bree said. "Besides, I'm not leaving here until I know that Lloyd is okay as well as the other people who were injured today. Plus, the police chief wants me to stick around in case she has any more questions. So this conversation is over."

Emerson shook his head, his beady little eyes narrowing as if he was trying to come up with another way to convince Bree to change her mind. Finally, he said, "I think you're making a mistake."

"You've made that clear. And I've also made myself clear."

He let out a sigh and took a step back. "Fine. Have it your way. Since I know you're all safe and sound here, I'm going to get back to my place and turn in for the night. I'm going to need to make some calls. I had already set up some studio time for you. And there are some new songs that I want you to listen to."

"Please tell me they weren't written by Hans Jennings?"

"What's wrong with Hans Jennings? He's a hit maker."

"His songs are horrible."

"Horrible? They're on every radio across the country right now, number one hits. The songs have helped make your career."

"Everybody knows they have no depth. Anyone could sing them. The lyrics don't reflect me, my stories, or what I believe in."

"This isn't about reflecting you. This is about making a career."

"I know. But making a career on shallow songs that reflect nothing about me at all seems like a wasted opportunity."

"It's late. You just need to get some sleep."

Emerson stepped toward the door. "I'll talk to you in the morning."

And with that, he stormed away.

Dez watched him leave. When the door had slammed, he turned back to Bree. She sat on the couch with her arms crossed, shaking her head as if disgusted with the whole conversation.

Finally, she rose and paced back over toward the breakfast bar where she'd left her dinner. Dez had made a phone call, and one of his friends had delivered their meals about forty minutes later. Bree hadn't touched hers yet and, no doubt, it was cold by now. But she didn't complain as she took a bite.

Dez walked closer. "He seems like a piece of work."

"You can say that again." She rolled her eyes.

"Is he always like that?"

"Yes, as a matter of fact, he is. But he's supposed to be one of the best in the business. Everyone tells me how lucky I am." Bitterness edged her words.

"I have to give you kudos for standing up for yourself."

"I haven't always done so. I should've started to put my foot down much earlier. It's just, in the beginning, you're so anxious to see things happen that you'll say yes to nearly anything. I mean, not *anything* anything. I have my standards. I have a little brother and two sisters who look up to me, so I try to be a good example to them. But I have let my manager make far too many calls in my life already."

"Better late than never you realize that then, right?"

"Yeah, I guess you could say that."

"Just curious—where is your manager staying?" Dez leaned against the counter as they chatted.

"I think his house is about five or six down from this one."

"Do you always stay in separate locations?"

"Usually, we're in a hotel, and we each have our own rooms. It's a little different here since there are no hotels on the island. So the band has their own place, the crew has their own place, and then my manager and I also have our own places."

"You always stay alone?"

"Normally, my assistant stays with me, but her mom is having surgery this week. She's not with me right now." Bree paused, holding the burger in front of her. "Why are you asking?"

"Just trying to get a feel for how all this works. Will you stay here for a while? How about the rest of your band?"

"The rest of the band probably won't stay. I don't

see any reason why they should. Like I said, this was the end of our tour. They have some well-deserved time off coming up."

"Good to know."

Dez was trying to get a feel for what he'd gotten himself into. Though it wasn't his job to figure out who was behind today's shooting, he couldn't help but think through the possible suspects.

The most likely one seemed to be the crazy fan from earlier. However, that man had been escorted away from the concert right before the gunfire occurred. That pretty much ruled him out.

Dez had no doubt that there was more than one person who could be responsible, who could be obsessed with Bree Jordan.

That's what made all of this even scarier.

That and the fact that there was no evidence to show how someone had gotten into the house earlier to leave that note. No scratch marks on the windows. No doors that had been jimmied.

Nothing.

That meant the person had the code to get inside.

And that meant the person could be someone close to Bree.

POLICE CHIEF CASSIDY CHAMBERS leaned back in her office chair and squeezed her eyes shut for a moment.

She hadn't had a break all day today. In fact, this whole week had been crazy with the music festival being in town. The director of tourism for Lantern Beach had thought this three-day event would be a great way to bring people to the island during the off-season.

The move had been risky since the weather was always iffy on Lantern Beach in March. Sometimes it could be bitterly cold, and other times it felt like summer. They had been lucky because the weather this week had been in the sixties, which made it perfect for the festival.

In total, they'd had ten different bands come into town. Bree Jordan had been the obvious headliner. In fact, Cassidy was surprised that the woman had even agreed to come to such a small venue, especially considering her star status. Bree sold out venues wherever she went.

A majority of the island's residents had decided to leave the island during the festival, choosing instead to rent out their homes to visitors through various online programs. The island wasn't usually this crowded in March, but right now it was at capacity, similar to the peak months of July and August.

Some people had even come over by ferry in the mornings and then left in the evenings because there was nowhere for them to stay. Knowing this, they'd planned the concerts to end early. The last ferry left at seven.

It was great to see the economy booming, but, after what had happened earlier today, Cassidy wasn't sure if this music festival would be a positive or negative for the island.

Reports about what had happened were all over the news right now. Not exactly the hype that Lantern Beach wanted. Bad press was becoming all too common here.

Uncountable law enforcement agencies were now involved in this. Cassidy was so thankful that no one had been killed. It would have been so easy for that to happen.

The marine police and Coast Guard had been searching continuously for the boat. Finally, they discovered a Bayliner abandoned at a dock on the west side of the island. It had been stolen from a vacation home earlier in the day, but the owner hadn't been around to report it. Bullet casings had been found onboard.

But, whoever the gunman was, he was long gone. They had searched the island looking for him. However, since they did not have a positive ID on the man, it was going to be hard to locate him.

Cassidy didn't like the sound of this. A crew from the North Carolina State Bureau of Investigation was on their way, and Cassidy wouldn't be surprised if the FBI ended up getting involved in this as well.

Someone knocked at the door to her office, and she looked up to see her husband, Ty, standing there. Her day, if only for just a moment, felt brighter.

He stepped forward and planted a quick kiss on her cheek before saying, "You look tired."

"I am. And I don't know what time I'm going to be able to leave tonight. For that matter, I don't even know if I *will* be able to leave tonight."

"It's been crazy today, hasn't it?" He sat across from her and placed a container of food on her desk.

"To say the least." She peered at the container. "What's this?"

"Some leftover shepherd's pie. I warmed it before I came. I figured you hadn't taken any time to eat."

"It looks delicious." She pulled off the lid, took a

bite, and began giving him a brief rundown on the updates, which weren't many.

"I guess the Blackout guys are busy now?" Cassidy asked. "Did I hear they've been hired to maintain security for Bree?"

"That's right. We went over earlier to talk about security. I think Bree might give Dez a run for his money."

"What do you mean?"

"It's not often that Dez runs into somebody more charismatic and popular than he is."

That got a smile out of Cassidy. "True. I can't argue with that. You think Dez will ever settle down? I know he has the reputation of being a playboy."

"I think when he finds the right person, he'll have no problem moving forward. He's not a bad guy. He just hasn't found the right woman for him yet."

"Well, I hope everything goes well with his assignment."

Just then, Cassidy's phone buzzed. It was one of her officers, Braden Dillinger.

"Chief, we just got a report about a body."

Her spine stiffened. Those were not the words she wanted to hear. "A body?"

Ty's gaze met hers.

"Some late-night partiers were walking the beach when they found him. He'd been shot. They found his body on the beach about a block away from Bree Jordan's rental. You'll want to get down here."

CHAPTER TEN

BREE FINISHED HER BURGER. Even though it was only lukewarm by the time she ate it, she had to admit it hit the spot.

She tried to relax, knowing that a security system had been installed and that Dez and Griff were both here. But she couldn't bring herself to let down her guard. Too much had happened, and there was too much on the line right now.

Just when she started thinking about what she might do next—a warm bath was at the top of her list—her doorbell rang.

Dez and Griff both tensed and reached for their weapons.

"Stay with her," Dez ordered Griff.

Griff stayed close while Dez went down to the

front door and pulled it open. A moment later, Bree heard Chief Chambers' voice drift up the stairs.

"I wasn't expecting to see you here," Dez said.

"I was hoping to talk to Bree." The chief's voice carried through the house.

The police chief stepped into the living room a moment later, a somber expression on her face. "I need to have a word with you, Ms. Jordan."

Dez pointed at the dining room table. "Have a seat."

A moment later, they were all seated there, with the exception of Griff, who remained on guard near the stairs.

"What's going on?" Bree rubbed her hands together, trying to cover her nerves. The task felt impossible, though.

"A body was found on the beach. A man."

Bree's eyes widened. "What? Who?"

Cassidy pulled up her phone and showed Bree the picture.

She gasped as the man's familiar features came into focus. Blond hair. Pale skin. "That's the man who was always following me from concert to concert, who always tries to catch me alone."

"Correct. We brought him in earlier but didn't

have enough to hold him. Do you know much about the man?"

"No, I don't even know his name. I never asked. My manager said it was better if I didn't give him any attention. That if I did the man would take it as a sign that I wanted more."

Chief Chambers nodded. "Probably good advice. Do you know anything else about him? Has he ever appeared dangerous toward you?"

Bree remembered all the encounters she'd had with the man before. "No, he was always eager to talk to me. I'm not going to lie, he scared me on more than one occasion. But he never actually touched me or did anything that came close to harming me."

"Good to know," the police chief said.

"How did he die?" Bree's voice cracked.

"He was shot. On the beach. Point blank."

Bree squeezed the skin between her eyes. "I can't believe this. Where was he found?"

"A couple of blocks south of here."

"Near my manager's house?"

"Is he staying six houses down?" the chief asked.

"Six houses to the south."

Cassidy nodded. "Yes, that's near where the body was found. I will need to talk to your manager."

"I'm sure he would be happy to answer any of

your questions. In fact, I'm kind of surprised he didn't come out when he saw all the commotion on the beach. I'm sure he's still awake."

"I'll need his number."

Bree rattled it off to Chief Chambers.

"Also, I need you to show me the threats you received," Chief Chambers continued. "Do you have them with you?"

"They're on my computer."

"Could you get it?"

"Of course." Bree left the room and returned a few minutes later. She pulled up the emails she'd received. She could hardly read them herself, though. Whenever she did, her stomach turned with revulsion.

She knew what they said. *You're going to die, and I'm going to have fun killing you. This world would be better off without people like you. Your life will be coming to an end—be ready.*

Then there were the photos. Photos where Bree's face had been scratched out with a black marker. Photos where a red line had been drawn across her neck. Of a puddle of blood that had been labeled "Bree's."

"I'm going to need copies of these." The chief

frowned. "I want to help you get to the bottom of this."

"I would love for someone to get to the bottom of this," Bree said. "I'm tired of living in fear."

"I'll do whatever I can to help," Dez said. "Nobody should be threatened like this."

The chief's gaze met Bree's. "I'm sure I don't need to tell you how serious this is."

"I almost wish I was in the dark about just how real all of this is. But I'm not." Even if she wanted to forget, those facts were driven home again and again.

"You have some of the best guys here watching out for you. In full disclosure, my husband is connected with the business, Blackout." Chief Chambers stood. "Since I didn't personally recommend these guys to you, there's no conflict of interest."

"That explains how you seem to know all of them," Bree said.

"And I would trust them with my life, so I know you're in good hands."

"That's good to know, at least."

"If you think of anything or need anything, call me." The police chief took a step toward the door. "In the meantime, try to get some sleep tonight."

As Bree watched the chief leave, she had a feeling that Chief Chambers would not be taking that advice herself. It seemed like law enforcement here had a long night ahead of them.

"STUFF like this isn't supposed to happen on Lantern Beach," Dez told Griff.

Bree had gone to take a long bath, which gave Griff and Dez a few minutes alone to talk. They stood in the hallway outside her room, still on guard.

"I know, it's crazy, isn't it?"

"I have to say, I thought that guy was our number one suspect," Dez said. "But since someone else got to him . . . I guess we're back at square one."

"Why would someone want to kill Bree?" Griff flipped his hand in the air, like the notion was ridiculous. "That's what I can't figure out. I can understand if someone wanted to be with her or give her attention. To kill her? That takes this to a whole different level."

"Maybe it's one of those 'if I can't have you no one can' type of things." Dez felt his muscles harden every time he thought about those threats. Bree's stalker was more than just a lovesick fan. This guy was a psychopath who wanted to see Bree dead.

The more he learned, the more this situation left him uncomfortable.

Griff crossed his arms and leaned against the wall. "I suppose that could be the case. I just feel like there's a lot more here that we haven't even begun to uncover yet."

"You're probably right." Dez shook his head, knowing his thoughts were getting him nowhere right now. "Listen, Griff, why don't you go ahead and get some sleep? That way we can trade off shifts later."

"You sure? I know you've had a long day."

"Yeah, I'm sure."

Dez had to admit that he was anxious to talk to Bree. He wanted to know more about her life, about who might be responsible for this. It wasn't that he didn't trust Cassidy and her crew to find answers. But Dez was here, and he had access to Bree. It seemed like he should use that to try to find some answers.

Griff made no effort to leave, so Dez paused. "Something on your mind?"

Griff let out a long breath and rubbed his jaw.

"Yeah, I guess you could say that. I keep thinking about Jason."

"Jason Perkins?"

Jason Perkins had worked as part of the crew for their SEAL team's former commander. It turned out Jason was also working for a deadly terrorist organization known as the Savages. He'd been feeding the terrorists information on the command's plans. Jason's betrayal had ultimately led to the death of their leader, Daniel Oliver.

After Daniel's wife, Elise, had discovered some information Daniel had hidden, she also became a target. Jason had followed her here, desperate to get his hands on the incriminating evidence. When that hadn't worked, he'd tried to kill her.

"I can't help but think that Jason couldn't have planned everything that happened here by himself," Griff said. "Jason wasn't the brightest guy around. To think that he tried to kill Elise and then tracked her down here, disguised himself . . . it's been bugging me lately."

Dez tried to keep an even expression. "Did you tell Colton?"

Griff shrugged again. "He just looks so happy now that he and Elise are together. I don't want to be paranoid."

Dez released his breath and decided to own up to his feelings on the matter. "To be honest, I've thought the same thing. I bet Colton has too. I'm not sure how much we can do, though, since we're not in the military anymore. If there is someone else pulling the strings, it will be almost impossible for us to get to him."

"I called my friend Anderson Bryant."

"He's still a SEAL, right?" From what Dez remembered about the man, he was a decent frogman, even taking a bullet for someone on his team once.

Griff nodded. "That's right. He's going to keep his eyes open."

"Maybe he'll discover something then."

"Yeah, maybe. I just don't want to see anyone else get hurt in the meantime."

"None of us do." Dez pressed his lips together in thought. "Let me know what you hear. I'll do the same."

Griff disappeared to his temporary bedroom, and, several minutes later, Bree emerged.

Dez's breath caught when he saw her. Bree always looked stunning. But, whenever he saw her on camera or onstage, her hair was always perfectly styled, her makeup heavy, and her outfits almost more like costumes.

Right now, in her black yoga pants and oversized sweatshirt, with her hair pulled back into a ponytail, she'd never looked so beautiful. She just looked so normal, so natural.

Dez forced himself to look away before he made her uncomfortable.

She flashed him a smile and then held up her phone as she walked past, as if to indicate she was talking to somebody.

Like a dutiful guard, he followed behind her as she headed down the hall. Dez was determined to keep an eye on Bree and this place, no matter the cost. He wasn't going to mess up again. Losing Daniel had been heart-wrenching enough. It had been Dez's job to cover him, and he'd failed.

"What happened is beyond horrible." Bree's voice floated back to him as she walked into the living room. "Thank you for your concern."

Dez couldn't hear what was being said on the other line, but, based on Bree's body language, it wasn't pleasant. She paused in the living room but didn't sit. Her body looked too stiff to do so.

"I'm not really sure why you want to see me now of all times. When I asked you to come see me a couple of months ago, you were too busy and had no room in your schedule."

Something else was said, something that had Dez more curious than he should be. He paused near the doorway, trying to remain a comfortable distance away and not invade her privacy.

"You really want to know what I think?" Bree let out a long breath and licked her lips. "I think you haven't made the headlines in a long time, and, now that you see what's happening to me, you see your chance to weasel back into my life. It's not going to happen."

Though the words had a bite, her voice was still soft, like she wanted to be forthright while still being kind. The trait—and effort—was admirable.

A few minutes later, Bree hit a button on the phone and tossed it on the couch. She sat on one of the blue cushions there and shook her head.

Dez contemplated if he should even acknowledge that he had heard her side of that conversation. He knew it wasn't his business, yet . . . Bree looked like she needed someone to talk to.

He would leave the ball in her court, he decided.

But curiosity burned inside him.

Bree Jordan fascinated him . . . and that was something he hadn't expected. Yet every time he saw her, he couldn't help but think about how Leah had broken his heart.

Dez had to remember that . . . because he never wanted to put himself in that position again. Nor could he live with himself if someone else died on his watch.

CHAPTER ELEVEN

BREE SHOOK HER HEAD AGAIN, all too aware that Dez had heard her talking to Mike Andrews. Her bodyguard stood near the doorway, a placid look on his face. His job wasn't to listen to her problems, but she had no one else here for her right now ... and he'd been kind earlier.

"Sorry you had to hear that." She pulled her legs beneath her.

She stared at the dark sky outside. Mike was on Pacific time, so it wasn't that late for him. Only 10:30. But here in North Carolina it was 1:30 in the morning, and she was exhausted. Yet she knew she wouldn't be able to sleep yet.

"That was Mike." Each recollection of their conversation made her fists tighten at her sides.

"Mike?"

She stared at him. She just assumed Dez would know who she was talking about. "Mike Andrews? The professional baseball player for the LA Dodgers?"

Realization spread through Dez's eyes. "*That* Mike Andrews. You're dating?"

"We've been on again, off again for the past eight months. Our publicist actually set us up. She thought if we dated each other it could do good things for both of our careers." She frowned as the words left her lips.

"And has it?"

"I don't know if it's done good things for my career or not, but I know it has done bad things to my psyche."

"That didn't sound like a fun conversation you just had."

"After not talking to me for a couple of months, he suddenly wants to come here so he can be with me?" Bree shook her head. "I don't buy that anymore. He just sees this as an opportunity to get more publicity for himself. I can't believe I wasted so much time with him. But finding love when you're famous . . . it's not as easy as one might think."

"If there's one piece of advice I'd give you it's that

when you find the person you're supposed to be with, you won't feel as miserable as you look right now. You should be lighting up every time you talk to him."

"Lighting up, huh?" She raised an eyebrow. "I like that. But I don't remember the last time I found myself 'lighting up' around a guy." Mostly she found herself questioning their motives, wondering if schedules could work together, and figuring out excuses why they'd never work out as a couple.

"You obviously haven't been around the right guy." Dez shrugged and offered an almost sly smile.

"I'll keep that in mind." Bree leaned back, feeling better. "All right, so you know about me and my love life or lack thereof. Now it's my turn. Are you married?"

"I am not." He remained straight-faced.

"You ever been married?"

"I have not."

He wasn't going to make this easy, was he? That didn't deter Bree. "Do you have a girlfriend?"

"I do not."

"Well, this conversation has been enlightening. Good talk." She flashed a wry smile.

Dez chuckled and shook his head. "Sorry. I'm not one to talk very much about dating. But no, I'm not dating anyone. Yes, I frequently go out on dates. I suppose I'm looking for that one, but I haven't found her yet. Until I do, I'm having fun."

Bree stared at him with all his endearing qualities. He was so good-looking that she almost didn't want to like the man. But he seemed so authentic that it was hard not to. However, guys like him had always been able to pull one over on her.

The charming, charismatic ones were her weakness.

"I'm sure you have broken a lot of hearts by doing that," she finally said.

"I'm always upfront. As soon as I know that a person is not the one for me, I break things off. I think I would be doing a disservice if I kept stringing the ladies along. But how will I know if I like them unless we go out a couple of times?"

"You sound convincing." He seemed like the type who had a long line of ladies waiting for him. Was he just using that reasoning as an excuse to justify his actions? In her experience—probably.

Dez studied her a moment, making no apologies about it. "You sound skeptical."

"Let's just say I've been around a lot of players in my life." Bree rolled her eyes, remembering all the guys who'd wanted to date her just to have a chance in the spotlight. There was nothing like being used to wake you up to the harsh realities of dating.

Her most recent ex was a case in point. With his baseball career fading, he'd suddenly become interested in accompanying Bree to every media-worthy event she'd attended.

He'd only wanted to pad his own popularity and to use Bree in the process.

How could she have been so stupid?

"Who said I was a player?" Dez looked offended—at least, mockingly so.

Bree shrugged, determined not to fall for his charm. "You give off that vibe."

"Are you talking about your love life or one of the songs that you sing?"

"Okay, I might sing a song called 'The Player,' but since I didn't write that and I don't even really like that song, no, that is *not* what I am talking about. I just get so tired of people using people." Her voice trailed.

"I would never want to use somebody." Dez's voice turned serious, and Bree knew she had struck a nerve.

"I'm sorry. I didn't mean to imply that."

"It's no problem." Dez stood. "I should go check out the rest of the house one more time."

As Bree watched him walk away, she felt like she'd just driven a wedge between them. Could you even drive a wedge if you'd only known the person for a few hours? Bree didn't know. But a sense of regret filled her.

It was silly, really. She had much bigger worries to think about right now. Starting with staying alive. That was what she needed to concentrate on.

LONG AFTER BREE went to bed, Dez's thoughts lingered on their conversation.

And they lingered on Leah.

It wasn't that he was still hung up on the woman. He wasn't. He had no desire to be with her again.

But Leah was one of the only women he'd ever let into his life . . . and she'd crushed his heart.

They'd met right after Dez became a SEAL. She was blonde and beautiful, the life of the party, the woman who lit up a room.

He'd fallen hard, and he'd fallen fast.

Dez had known he wanted to spend the rest of his life with her, and he'd worked up the nerve to finally tell her that. The anxiety had been strange for

Dez. He was always the confident one, the guy who didn't doubt his abilities.

Until he met Leah.

But he bought the ring, and he planned the night. When he'd popped the question . . . she'd laughed.

Yes, laughed.

She'd told him she wasn't looking for anything serious, especially not with a Navy SEAL. She'd assumed he felt the same way—that he'd only wanted a good time.

Except he hadn't felt that way.

As one final jab, she'd muttered something about Dez never being able to support her lifestyle while he was a SEAL. He couldn't even argue. SEALs didn't make that much money. It wasn't a job for someone who wanted to live rich.

And Leah had.

Leah had walked out of his life that day with a piece of his heart.

After losing her . . . Dez had realized he never wanted to put himself in that position again. Ever.

It was one of the reasons he liked to keep things with women shallow, to not get too close.

So why was Bree stirring up these feelings inside him? It made no sense.

She was just like Leah ...

That was what he kept telling himself, at least.

Both Leah and Bree were blonde, thin, beautiful. They turned every head in the room and could capture any heart they wanted.

It was all the more reason Dez should stay away.

Too bad that was easier said than done.

CHAPTER TWELVE

DEZ AND GRIFF had traded shifts at six a.m. so Dez could get a couple hours of shut-eye. It hadn't mattered. Dez couldn't sleep, and he'd risen by eight to shower and get ready.

At least the night had been quiet with no more emergencies.

As Dez wandered upstairs, he heard music ringing out. Not on a device, however. It was live.

He paused in the hallway before entering the living room. Sunlight filtered in through high windows, and the smell of coffee floated in the air. But it was Bree that caught his attention.

She sat on the couch with her guitar. A paper and pen were in front of her as she sang.

"Your love is like the ocean on a cloudless, sunny

day." Her smooth voice rang out, the kind of voice he could listen to all day.

This woman had some chops. He had to admit that he'd wondered if her talent was just overproduced, the kind sound engineers could manipulate.

It wasn't.

"And every time I feel it, I feel like I could run away. Run into forever. Run into the unknown. Run into a place where my dreams can be my own." Bree continued, obviously not hearing him come in.

The song painted Bree in a different light—again. The woman was constantly surprising him. But this song that Bree sang now was so raw, so natural. There were no pop vibes present, only earthy tones.

Just as last night, Bree wore casual clothes, no makeup, and her hair had been pulled away from her face. She looked normal—beautiful, but normal.

It was almost like she was a different person than she was onstage. He'd expected a diva, someone spoiled and demanding.

But Bree wasn't like that.

Dez took a step and cleared his throat, trying not to scare her. Immediately, the song ended, and Bree jerked her head toward him.

"I didn't mean to interrupt," he said.

"Oh, you're fine." Her shoulders relaxed. "I was just playing around."

"What was that song?" Dez asked, moving closer.

"It's just a little ditty I've been working on, as they say." She flashed him a soft, almost sad smile.

"Well, you should keep playing with it. It sounds really good."

She shrugged, put the guitar down by her side, and grabbed the cup of coffee she'd left on the table. "I'm not sure that my manager will agree with that."

She'd said that last night also. Their issues must run deep.

"What does he know?" Dez grabbed a cup of coffee before lowering himself into the chair across from her.

"Apparently, he knows a lot. He's a star maker, after all. That's what people call him."

"So he doesn't let you do any of your own stuff?" He took a sip of his coffee.

"No, he says the stuff I write doesn't fit my brand." She shrugged and twisted her lips, as if holding back a diatribe that revealed her true feelings.

"How does that even work? I don't know a lot about the music industry, but aren't you your own brand?"

She picked up her guitar again and ran her fingers down the strings, a frown on her face. "In theory. At least, I always envisioned that I would be. But Emerson discovered me and groomed me for this position. I had been singing at state fairs and church camps. But he saw something in me and paid out of his pocket to make me who I am today."

Something about the way Bree said the words made it sound like it wasn't necessarily a good thing.

"So he discovered you, groomed you, and eventually you got a record contract?"

She nodded. "Yes, that's the way it worked for me. There was a time when I felt like the luckiest girl in the whole world."

"And now?"

Bree shrugged, a far-off look in her eyes as she hugged the guitar against her. "I don't know. I'm trying to embrace what I've been given. But part of me feels like I've given up too much."

"What do you mean?" Dez couldn't seem to stop asking the questions. Hearing Bree's story was fascinating—and disconcerting at the same time.

She frowned and loosened her hold on the guitar. "I mean, when I decided to accept his offer, I was eighteen years old. Old enough to make my own choices. But my parents didn't agree with what I was doing. They thought Emerson would corrupt me and that all of this was a mistake. Long story short, they gave me an ultimatum. If I decided to continue on with Emerson, they didn't want anything to do with me."

Dez blanched as he tried to put himself in her shoes. "That's harsh."

She shrugged, a sad look on her face. "I don't think they really ever expected me to walk away from them. They probably figured I loved my brother and sisters too much. I miss them terribly. But my parents won't let them have anything to do with me. It's been six years since I left."

He could see the pain etched into her eyes, hear the sorrow in her voice. The sacrifices she'd made to get to where she was today were greater than he'd ever imagined. "Why did your parents think your manager was such a bad guy?"

"They'd seen some of the other acts that he discovered and created. Most of the girls ended up wearing skimpy outfits, doing provocative dances, and singing about things that were not wholesome, let's just say. They didn't want me to become that person."

"From what I can tell, you're not that person."

"I've chosen my battles. There are things I compromised on. Things like the kind of songs I sing. But there were other things that I couldn't compromise on, especially knowing I was setting an example for not only my siblings but for other young people out there."

"Seems like they would admire you for that."

She shrugged again. "I would like to think they would, but, as the saying goes, I made my bed and now I have to lie in it."

That's not what Dez thought about her story. More surprises kept popping up concerning Bree. She was nothing like Dez had expected, nor was this assignment.

As much as he would like to sit here all day and chat, pretending like this was just a casual hangout, Dez knew it was anything but. There was still a killer out there, and, whoever this person was, he had his sights set on Bree.

BREE PUSHED a stray hair behind her ear. She hadn't intended on opening up to Dez like she did. There was something about him that made him easy to talk to.

At one time in her life, if she'd seen someone as

good-looking as Dez, she would have been intimidated by him. At the least, she would have assumed he was superficial.

But Dez was proving to be the opposite of what she'd thought. He wasn't just brawny, he was a good listener.

Bree mentally shook her head. She couldn't let her thoughts go there. Dez was hired help, for goodness sake. He was probably just listening because it was his job.

Yet, in her line of work, there were very few people who really wanted to get to know her for her. Most people wanted to befriend Bree for who they *thought* she should be or what she could do for them. But the lack of close relationships in her life was beginning to take its toll.

Last night before going to bed, she'd talked to her assistant, Karen. Bree had numerous other messages from people trying to check on her. The outpouring of support was heartwarming, and she was thankful for it.

Karen had asked if she was coming back to LA soon. Bree had said no. She had no desire to go back to the grind. She'd rather stay here, where the ocean was soothing to her soul.

Bree let out a breath and glanced back at Dez. "Any updates?"

"I did talk to Cassidy—make that the Police Chief Chambers. They learned more about the victim. His name was Kyle Thompson, and he was from a small town in Louisiana. Apparently, he gave up his job in order to follow you from concert to concert."

"Great, it's like I have my own version of the Deadheads."

Dez flashed a smile. "I suppose you could look at it like that. He had a history of being obsessed with people he liked. One woman he'd worked with at an insurance agency filed a restraining order against him. There was no record of him actually being violent, only obsessive. But we both know what that can lead to."

"Yes, we do." Bree frowned. "But are there any leads as to who killed him? And who was behind the gunfire at the concert yesterday?"

"I know everyone is working on it, but, as far as I know, there aren't any leads. They have asked anybody who was at the concert yesterday to turn over any video footage so authorities can look at it. I know the North Carolina State Bureau of Investigation arrived last night, and they're helping with the investigation. The FBI is also on standby."

Bree rubbed her throat. "I suppose this latest info is all over the news."

Dez nodded, an almost apologetic look in his eyes. "It is."

"Good to know."

Just then, her phone rang. Bree looked at the screen and saw that it was Emerson. Dread pooled in her stomach.

"Excuse me a second." Bree stood and paced into the hallway for privacy.

"Bree, good morning. How are you feeling today?"

"About as well as can be expected."

"That's what I figured. Look, I'll cut right to the chase. I think you need to do a press conference."

She leaned with her hip against the wall. "Why do you think that?"

"You need to get ahead of this. I'm not sure how all of this will play out, but you need to let people know how hard this has been for you. I'm thinking we should set up a fund in your name to help out any of the victims with either their medical needs or counseling after the event."

"That's not a bad idea. I want to do anything I can to help."

"Plus, it will be good press."

Bree frowned. "That wasn't really the reason I was thinking about doing this."

"I know. That's why you have me. I think about things like this."

"When you say press conference, what are you thinking?" Bree held her breath, anxious to hear if they were on the same page.

"I'm thinking we go down to the police station and set a time and you give your side of the story."

Her side of the story? She didn't even know what that was yet. "There's not much else I can say except how deeply sorry I am for what happened."

"I think we can spin this. We can make this all about how you're against violence—"

"Wait. I don't want to spin this. It is what it is."

"If we handle this right, your popularity can soar."

"Emerson . . ."

"You should let me do what I do best here. I can arrange a conference at noon."

"Let me think about this first. I do have security issues to consider."

"Don't think too long."

"I'm not promising anything . . ."

She ended the call and glanced at Dez. Doing a press conference was the last thing Bree wanted to do, especially if her manager expected her to spin this to fit some sort of agenda.

She really did need to think this through. Because she was tired of making bad choices.

<h1 style="text-align:center">CHAPTER THIRTEEN</h1>

BREE'S BANDMATES stopped by that morning. Bobby Dee was her drummer, Stan was her bass player, and Marlin played lead guitar. As they chatted together in the living room, Dez pulled out his phone and did a quick internet search for the Savages.

He'd like to believe they were out of his life for good. But, for the sake of his country, he couldn't bury his head in the sand.

No results came up.

He frowned. Why was the government keeping their threats quiet? It didn't make sense. Sure, mass panic would do no one any good. But the Savages weren't even on the average American's radar.

Everything had been so surreal lately that Dez felt on edge.

It was probably nothing.

That's what he hoped, at least.

But in his life, things were rarely that easy.

AN HOUR LATER, Bree's band left her place. They had been a nice distraction from everything else going on. It had been good to be around people who shared her pain, who understood. They were all in shock right now. They would be for a while.

Stretching her legs, Bree went to grab her computer from an office area that had been set up off the main room. When she stepped into it, she saw Griff sitting there.

He held something in his hands, but it was the frown on his face that she noticed the most. What exactly was he looking at?

"I didn't mean to interrupt." She took a step back.

He straightened, as if she'd caught him off guard. The next instant, he slipped the paper—it almost looked like a photo—into his pocket and his melancholy expression disappeared.

"You're not interrupting." He started to rise. "I can get out of your way."

"No need to do that. Let me just grab my computer." Bree pointed to the laptop on the desk there.

He nodded and moved out of the way as she grabbed the device. A moment later, Bree escaped back into the living room, sat on the couch, and opened her laptop.

She wasn't sure exactly what she was doing or what she was looking for. Maybe she just needed to pass the time until she could figure out what decision to make about Emerson's proposal.

Bree was about to drink the poison, she supposed.

That's what she called it when she watched the bad press. When she read the bad reviews. When she chose to let those voices get inside her head.

As she pulled up the search bar, Bree's fingers lingered on the keys. She knew she shouldn't do it. But, despite that, she typed her own name there. The next instant, pages and pages of results appeared. Most of the recent ones were about the concert.

Bree clicked on the first video she came to. It had been taken by someone in the audience and showed Bree onstage, singing to the cheering crowd.

She had to admit that she was pretty good at

faking it. To watch this video, nobody would know about her doubts and misgivings.

Then, all of a sudden, the camera shifted. Shots rang out. People ran. Screams erupted.

Bree closed her eyes, those terrible moments replaying in her head. Every time she heard the gun going off, she flinched, feeling like she was right there again.

A shadow appeared beside her and pushed down the screen on her laptop until it closed. "You don't need to watch that."

She looked up and saw Dez standing there. He frowned as he stared at her, yet compassion stretched through his gaze.

She crossed her arms, knowing his words were true. "Yesterday still seems surreal."

"I know. But watching it isn't going to do anything for you." He sat down beside her.

She glanced over at him, studying his expression. "What do you think? Should I have a press conference?"

Dez shrugged and let out a long breath. "I think you should do what you want to do."

"I don't want my manager to control the narrative." Bree didn't trust Emerson enough to let him do that—not in this situation, at least. He knew entertainment. But could he truly navigate tragedy?

"Then don't let him," Dez said.

"But I feel like I need to do something." Bree sat up straighter. "What if I released a video on my VideoStream channel?"

Dez shrugged before nodding. "That would certainly be one way to control the narrative. Plus, I have to admit that I'm not 100 percent comfortable putting you in front of people right now. Not while this gunman is still out there."

"That's what I think I will do then. I will make a video announcement myself. Plus, it will give me something to do today." Satisfaction zinged through her. She finally had a solution she could live with.

Bree opened her computer again. As she did, a notification popped up.

There were pictures there. Lots of pictures.

She sucked in her breath when she saw the details. There were photos of her. With Dez. Here in Lantern Beach.

In one, they ran from the clinic to a waiting car. In another, he shielded her as they walked into her rental house. In the third, Dez escorted her from the stage at the shooting.

Her stalker was still on this island. He was

patiently waiting to finish the task that he had started.

Was Dez a target now also?

The thought caused her head to swirl until she felt like she might pass out.

CHAPTER FOURTEEN

"NOW THAT YOU have had time to sleep on it, is there anybody at all you can think of who might be behind this?" Chief Chambers held a pen and paper in her hands as she waited for Bree's answer. She'd also brought an extra-large cup of coffee with her.

She'd obviously had a long, sleepless night.

The police chief had come to Bree's house—again—and now sat across from her at the dining room table. Dez lingered close, listening to the conversation. He wanted the answer to that question just as much as anybody. Though he was being paid to protect and not investigate, he still wanted to figure out who was behind all this.

Bree shook her head, her oversized sweatshirt pulled down over her hands and one knee pulled to her chest. "That's all I've been thinking about as well. I just don't know who."

"There's no one who has had some kind of beef with you?" Cassidy reframed the question.

Bree rubbed the side of her face and drew in a long breath, almost appearing like the question burdened her. "There are always people who have a beef with me. I get plenty of hate mail. I don't even know how to narrow it down."

"Has there been any one person in particular who's been consistent?"

Bree frowned. "I suppose there have been a couple of people who've been particularly pushy. But you're going to need to talk to my manager about them. I finally started filtering everything through him and my assistant. I couldn't handle reading some of the emails anymore. They were too harsh."

"But you got some threats through your email, correct? That's what you mentioned yesterday." Chief Chambers tapped her pen against the paper and waited.

"Correct. They went to my personal account. Local police tried to check the sender's address but they had no luck."

"How did someone get your email address?" Dez shifted, her answer grabbing his attention.

Bree shrugged. "That's a great question. I've been too busy to figure that out."

"Anybody else?" the chief asked. "Any fellow musicians?"

"No, there's no one—" Bree stopped midsentence.

"What is it?" Dez straightened. "You remembered someone, didn't you?"

"This is probably nothing." Bree shook her head, as if trying to talk herself out of it.

"Let us be the judge of that," Cassidy said. "Tell us what you're thinking."

Bree sighed and rubbed the side of her face again. "About three months ago, when my latest single released, another singer accused the man who wrote my song of stealing it from her. I wasn't directly involved in the conflict, but, since I sang the song, I kind of was."

"What was this songwriter's name?" Cassidy raised her pen.

"His name is Hans Jennings. He's based out of LA, I believe."

"And who was the one who accused him of stealing the song?"

"Trixie Dare."

The chief stared at her. "You do know that Trixie

Dare sang the day before you, right?"

Bree nodded. "I suppose I may have heard she was here or seen it on one of the brochures. I didn't really think anything of it. Should I have? I mean, I didn't get here until the morning the day of my concert. I figured the other bands were already gone. Either way, I didn't really have time to be sociable."

"I'm just gathering information." Cassidy took a long sip of her coffee. "What else happened with the situation?"

Bree hugged her leg to her chest. "It was mostly between Hans and Trixie. I tried not to get involved."

"Did Trixie ever talk to you about it?" Dez wanted to know more information so he could get to the bottom of this. He realized that Bree didn't want to throw anyone under the bus—and he could appreciate that—but Bree's life was on the line. This was no time to be polite.

"She did have a couple of conversations with me about it. She told me I should renounce Hans and not use any more of his songs until this was resolved. She told me I was putting myself in a bad position."

"And what did you tell her?" Chief Chambers took another long sip of coffee.

"I let Emerson handle it. I suppose I let him handle a lot of those messy things in my life. I told her I didn't have anything to do with it, and that while Hans' song and hers did have a few similarities, it didn't sound alike enough to justify plagiarism to me."

Emerson sure did have his hand in much of Bree's life. Too much, if you asked Dez.

"Did it go to court?" Dez asked.

"Trixie talked about filing a lawsuit, but I never heard anything of it." Bree shrugged. "I figured it had passed."

"She is not a very big act," Cassidy said. "In fact, she opened for somebody else at this festival, if I remember correctly."

"Her career hasn't taken off like mine, but she did just sign with a small label," Bree said. "I've seen it enough in my own life. People are so desperate to make it, to become famous, that they'll do anything to get that attention."

Attention . . . ? Was the desire for fame the root cause of all these problems? There was a lot to be said for just being happy with where you were and what you had. Leah breaking up with him was a blessing. He could have never made her happy, though he couldn't see it at the time.

"Do you think she came up with all this just to get attention?" Dez asked.

"I wouldn't go as far as to say that." Bree shrugged, almost looking guilty as she nibbled on her bottom lip. "But the thought did cross my mind."

"I think I'm going to need to pay this Trixie Dare a visit." The chief stood. "I wonder if she's still on the island. I'll talk to the festival coordinator and see what I can find out."

Bree shifted again, as if uncomfortable. She'd had another thought, Dez realized. But she was hesitant to share it.

"There is one other thing," Bree finally started. "In no way am I trying to point fingers. But I do know that Trixie has three older brothers, and they're all avid outdoorsmen. They would definitely know how to use a gun."

Cassidy and Dez exchanged a look.

Maybe they had their first real lead.

THAT CONVERSATION with Chief Chambers had left Bree feeling drained. And guilt-ridden. She had tried to be fair in everything she said. She didn't want to blame anybody. Yet, whoever was behind this couldn't get away with it either.

She hoped Trixie understood why her name had come up.

As Chief Chambers turned to leave, the police chief paused near Dez. "I don't suppose you'll be able to make Austin and Skye's party tonight."

"No, sorry. Duty calls. But please give Austin and Skye my apologies."

"Don't miss it because of me," Bree said.

Surprise flashed through Dez's eyes before he waved her off. "I don't mind staying here."

"I can go with you." Bree didn't know where the words had come from. Yes, she was craving normalcy. Was she so desperate for it that she was trying to insert herself into Dez's social calendar?

"I'm not sure that would be a good idea." Dez shook his head.

"I'm not trying to invite myself. I'm really not. But I also don't want to sit here all day. I might as well be in prison if I have to do that."

Dez and Chief Chambers glanced at each other.

"It will be a small group of people," Chief Chambers said. "It should be safe."

Dez turned back to her and shrugged. "If you really want to go, I'm sure we can make that happen."

"Only if I'm not imposing."

"I'm sure they would love to have you," the chief said. "In fact, I happen to know that Skye is a big fan."

"Then I look forward to meeting her."

After the police chief left, Bree turned to Dez. "I'm going to post my video now. Afterward, I would like to go see Lloyd at the clinic. Can you make that happen?"

"I'm sure I can."

She nodded. "Great. Give me thirty minutes, and I'll be ready."

But would she ever truly be ready to go out in public again? Because staying inside the walls felt safe. But, if she did that, then whoever was sending her these threats would win.

And she couldn't let that happen.

CHAPTER FIFTEEN

LLOYD LOOKED BETTER TODAY. Bree was glad to see it. It was a little bit of good news in a sea of bad news. He had even joked with her some about ways they could make Emerson mad. One of Lloyd's favorite things to do was to aggravate the man.

Bree had been here at the clinic for the past hour. Lloyd was with the doctor when she'd arrived, so she'd taken some time to visit the other patients. They'd seemed appreciative—and all of them were doing well and were slated to be released later today.

After visiting with Lloyd for about twenty minutes, Bree decided to broach the question that had lingered in her mind. "Lloyd, before I left yesterday, you said something about keeping an eye on the people closest to me. What did you mean?"

His eyebrows knit together. "I said that? I must have been delusional. I don't know."

"You really don't remember?"

He shook his head. "I don't."

"And it doesn't ring any bells?"

"I'm sorry, Bree. I was probably out of it because of all the drugs they gave me. Sorry to freak you out for no reason."

Bree wanted to press harder, but she didn't want to stress him out—not in his current state. Instead, she nodded and turned to go.

Maybe she would ask him again later.

Just as Bree looked over her shoulder to say goodbye, she nearly collided with Lloyd's girlfriend, Jill. The woman had ashy blonde hair that fell below her shoulders, tanned skin, and was painfully thin. Early wrinkles around her lips made it clear she was a smoker, as did her raspy voice.

Bree started to greet the woman. Before she could, Jill smacked her across the face.

Bree held her cheek, pain spreading across her skin and surprise reverberating in her head.

"Jill!" Lloyd said.

"This is all your fault." Jill didn't seem to hear him. Instead, she nearly growled as she scowled at Bree. "I told him he shouldn't go on tour with you."

"How is this her fault, Jill?" Lloyd asked, sounding a bit helpless in his hospital bed with various tubes and monitors hooked up to him.

Bree saw Dez hovering in the doorway. He was ready to act if the woman tried to strike again. She motioned for him to stand down. She could handle this.

"Controversy follows her wherever she goes." Jill threw another accusing look at Bree. "She should have looked after her band members more."

"You know I love my band." Bree wasn't sure what Jill was talking about. She'd never acted like she was above the other people on her team.

Anger flashed in Jill's hazel eyes. "Then why don't you pay them what they are worth?"

"Pay them what they're worth . . . ? What do you mean?" This was the first time Bree had ever heard anything about it. Did Jill even know what she was talking about?

"You're raking in the big bucks, and you're paying your band barely enough to live on. I'm better off getting my alimony check than I am getting married to Lloyd—you should be ashamed of yourself."

"Jill . . ." Lloyd warned again.

"I don't have anything to do with how much

they're paid. I had no idea they were underpaid." Bree glanced at Lloyd. "Is that true?"

He didn't say anything for a moment before sighing. "I was promised we'd get paid more when we did the second leg of your tour. Emerson negotiated the fee. He just didn't tell us about the hidden costs and expenses that would be deducted from it."

Bree lowered her head. "Why didn't you say anything to me about it? I would have fought to give you guys more money."

"I didn't say anything about it because I don't think Emerson is paying you what you deserve either."

Bree froze. "What do you mean?"

"There are rumors about the way he treats his artists and the way the contracts are drawn up. He's a one-man show. He manages you. Helps produce you. He owns the record label. I have a sneaking suspicion that he's bringing in the majority of money for himself."

Bree's heart pounded in her ears. "Do you think he would do that?"

"You and I both know him well enough to know that he's not a Boy Scout."

"I can't argue with that. But I didn't know he would sink this low."

"Listen, you have enough on your mind right now," Lloyd said. "We can deal with the pay thing later. Jill, you need to apologize."

Jill crossed her arms and shook her head. "You almost got killed for this woman. I am not apologizing."

"You know I would never purposely do anything to put them in danger," Bree said.

Jill said nothing. There was nothing that Bree could say to her right now that would make this situation better. But she hated the thought that Jill blamed her.

With a final wave to Lloyd, Bree stepped from the room. The last thing she had wanted to do was to bring more drama into Lloyd's life . . . it was time to get out of here.

DEZ'S MUSCLES were poised to act. The situation that had just played out in Lloyd's room made him uncomfortable, to say the least. That woman should have never touched Bree. But it was more than that. It sounded like Emerson had some shady practices going on and that Bree was in the middle of them.

As she stepped into the hallway, Dez leaned closer. "Are you okay?"

She touched her cheek again, still looking flushed. "I'll be fine. Just taken by surprise."

He wanted to ask her more questions, and he probably would. But not here. There were too many people around.

"Maybe we should get you out of here."

"That sounds like a good idea," Bree said.

But just as she said the words, a figure flew around the corner. Dez braced himself . . . until he saw it was Emerson. The man's face was red and his nostrils flared. He was obviously upset about something.

"You posted a video?" He stopped in front of Bree. "Without even telling me?"

"I thought it would be a good way to express myself and to say how sorry I feel about everything that happened. It seemed more personal than a press conference."

"You should've run it by me first."

"I just wanted to make a video, to let people see who I really was and how I was really feeling. I didn't want anything rehearsed."

"Well, that was a big mistake. These things need to be perfectly executed."

"It sounds to me like you're a control freak," Dez said.

Emerson looked up at him, his nostrils still flaring. "I don't think we are paying you to be a part of this conversation."

"I want him to stay." She touched Dez's arm, letting him know that he was wanted here.

"I think you're getting a little too big for your britches."

She tilted her head, her voice still gentle as she said, "Because I'm making my own choices? I should've been making choices for far longer than I obviously have."

"What does that mean?"

"What's this I hear about the band being underpaid? And you not telling the Lantern Beach police about my stalker? They would've had more security at the concert if they had known."

His eyes widened before his gaze hardened again. "It's easy to think that you have all the answers, but until you're in my shoes you can't possibly know what I do. I am doing what I think is best for your career. I guess I've done pretty well so far, haven't I? You were on six magazine covers this year, had twenty-one TV appearances, fifty-two concerts, and two number one hits. Do you think you did that all by yourself?"

"I'm not saying that you haven't helped me." Bree softened her voice. "Everyone knows that's not true. But when this is over, we need to have a long talk."

"Do you think you would be anything without me?" Emerson's voice came out with a tremble as he stared at her with accusation in his eyes.

Before Bree could respond, Dez's phone buzzed, and he looked at the screen.

"It looks like we have more problems than this to talk about right now," Dez said. "People are responding to your video. They are *really* responding to it. Most of it is good. But look at this."

He showed Bree the screen. Someone had posted a comment beneath it. Bree's face had been photoshopped onto a dead body—one with a bullet hole through the skull.

It looked real. All too real.

And the message was clear: someone wanted Bree to die.

CHAPTER SIXTEEN

CASSIDY KNOCKED at the door to a small cottage two blocks down the beach from Bree's place. A moment later, Trixie Dare answered. The woman was in her mid-twenties with stark black hair, pale skin, and a cold gaze.

She stared at Cassidy, tilting her head and narrowing her eyes as if she resented being disturbed.

"Can I help you? Did someone lose a cat or something?" Her voice came out with a bite.

Cassidy stuffed down her irritation. "I'm Police Chief Cassidy Chambers. I came because I have a few questions about the incident yesterday here on the island."

"I wasn't at that concert. I don't know what you could possibly want to talk to me about."

Cassidy raised her hand before the woman could close the door on her. "If you could just give me a few minutes."

The woman stared at her another moment before finally nodding and opening the door wider. "Fine. Come in. But I'm in the middle of writing a song, and you're messing with my mojo."

Cassidy stepped into the house but remained close to the door. She didn't want to take up any more time than necessary. But she did want some answers.

"Now, what's this about?" Trixie crossed her arms.

"It's about a song that you claim Hans Jennings stole from you."

The woman's eyes narrowed even more. "That's because he *did* steal it from me. I played it at a song-writing competition, and he was one of the judges. A year later, it comes out and he's claiming it as his own. Sure, he changed a few things. Enough to make it virtually his own. But most of that song was mine."

"Did you blame Bree Jordan for that?"

"Did I blame Bree? No. Why would I?"

"So you didn't confront her about it?"

"Is that what she told you?" Trixie's hip jutted out as outrage stretched through her voice.

"That's not important. Please check the attitude and just answer the question." Why couldn't anything be simple?

Trixie sighed. "I told her that she shouldn't be associated with someone who was a thief. If you want to call that a confrontation then so be it. I was trying to help her out, though."

Cassidy definitely felt some animosity in the air. "Are you jealous of Bree? I understand that you both started in the music business around the same time, and her career took off while yours did not."

"Of course I'm not jealous of her." Trixie scoffed. "I want to do my own songs. Not stuff that these other people have written. She is so mass-produced that I don't even know how she lives with herself."

This was a woman who had opinions and wasn't afraid to share them. Sometimes Cassidy found that to be admirable and other times annoying. This was one of the annoying times.

"Despite that mass production, as you call it, she is doing well for herself," Cassidy said.

"If I do well for myself, I want it to be on my own terms." Trixie raised her chin.

"Where were you yesterday during Bree's concert?"

Trixie's eyes widened. "I was sleeping. Why? Is that a crime?"

"I'm just gathering information," Cassidy said. "Is there anyone here with you?"

"My band left right after I played."

"Anyone else?"

Trixie frowned, as if she didn't want to answer the question. Finally, she said, "Two of my brothers are here."

"Where are they now?"

"Fishing again. It's kind of their thing . . ." Trixie pulled her arms tighter across her chest, as if she didn't like where this was going.

"And where were your brothers yesterday during the concert?"

"They were out fishing. That's what they like to do. It's how I convinced them to come."

"Deep-sea fishing or out on the sound?"

"Deep-sea." Trixie's lips barely moved as she said the words.

"Did they charter a boat, by chance?"

"No, they rented one. You can't possibly believe that they were the ones behind the shooting?"

Cassidy chose not to answer that question.

"What I'm wondering is whether you feel so much vengeance toward Bree Jordan that you wanted to take her out."

Trixie's arms fell to her side, and all of the tension in her face dissolved with slack—and maybe a touch of fear. "My brothers would never do that. I might be angry, but I am not *that* angry."

Cassidy wasn't so sure about that. "We need you to stick around, just in case we have any more questions for you."

"DO you want to go back to the house?" Dez asked as they climbed into the car he'd borrowed after leaving the clinic.

He sensed that Bree was still reeling from the conversations she'd just had—as well as seeing that manipulated photo showing her dead body with a bullet hole through the forehead.

His stomach churned with unease at the thought of it.

"I'd love to grab a bite to eat," she said. "Maybe to-go."

"I know just what we can do. I'll call my favorite place with a to-go order, and I'll get the waitress to run the food out to us so we never have to leave the car."

"That sounds perfect. I'm not quite ready to go out in public and face anybody else. So far today, me going out in public hasn't been a very good idea." She frowned and tucked herself against the seat.

Sympathy pressed on him as he put the car in Drive. "I am sorry for what happened back there. I know that had to be uncomfortable for you."

"To say the least. I thought I was doing the right thing by letting Emerson handle the business side of things. I tried not to worry myself over those details. But I can see now that was a mistake."

He started down the road, trying to find the right words to comfort her. "You're new to the business. I know you're still learning the ropes. I'm sure this is all normal."

"Maybe my family was right when they said that this whole business would make me into a different person."

He glanced at her, sensing a surprising broken-ness. "I would say you've stayed true to yourself pretty well."

She glanced at him, something close to gratitude in her gaze. "You really think so?"

"I know you have to be an entertainer when

you're onstage. But when you're offstage, you're very real. Very relatable and down-to-earth. I think that's something to be proud of. A lot of people would have let fame get to their heads by now."

A smile feathered across her face. "Well, thank you for the vote of confidence. If only everyone felt that way."

"I think the video you did today was a good start. It lets people see who you really are. It was from the heart and a much better idea than the press conference that Emerson wanted to schedule."

She rubbed her arms and glanced at him. "Do you think that the killer sent those pictures? And posted that photo of me in response to my video?"

"It's a definite possibility. Someone is trying very hard to send you a message. He's doing an outstanding job."

Bree let out an airy, cynical laugh. "Yes, he is."

They pulled up to a restaurant called The Crazy Chefette. The place looked cheerful with its pink and yellow exterior, and it was a local favorite.

Dez had called about their food. As they waited, he glanced around. Two news vans were in the lot.

Calling in the order to-go had definitely been a good idea. He couldn't afford to let down his guard.

A few minutes later, a waitress brought out two

bags and two drinks. The smell of toasted bread and homemade potato chips filled the vehicle. He handed Bree a sack, along with the lemonade she'd ordered.

"This is what the restaurant is famous for," Dez explained. "It's a grilled cheese and peach sandwich. Try it. You might like it."

"I'm a closet foodie, so this actually sounds really good." She opened the paper wrapper and picked up the sandwich, examining it for a moment. "Listen, instead of driving back to the house, would you mind driving me around the island? Do you think it would be safe?"

Dez glanced around. "I don't see a ton of people out and about today, so we could probably arrange that. Where do you want to go?"

"I just want to see more of this place. Usually, when I go to all of these new towns, I'm in and out. I don't really get to visit local sites or experience anything. And seeing and experiencing new places is one of my favorite things ever."

"I'd be happy to give you a tour. I've only been here a few months, but I think I know enough to show you around."

She took a bite of her sandwich as they pulled away. "Where are you from?"

"My mom is from Cuba, and my dad is from Miami. They both still live down in southern Florida."

"You seem like somebody who might be from down that way. It's a great city. I really enjoyed my concert there."

"It is a pretty great place. A lot of cultures there."

She held her sandwich in front of her, as if displaying it as a point of interest. "And this sandwich is fantastic."

"See? I told you. I've got great taste."

"A man who knows his strengths. I can't argue about that." She guided the conversation back to the more personal. "So, do you talk to your parents a lot?"

"I talk to my mama every Saturday morning. I call her at nine o'clock sharp so we can catch up."

She smiled and took another bite. "So you're a mama's boy?"

"No shame in that."

Bree let out another laugh. "No shame at all."

Dez pointed out several places to her, including the lighthouse and the Pamlico Sound. He shared some trivia about each place. They ended their drive at the harbor area.

"It's not much to look at, but it's beautiful in its

own way," Dez said. "In fact, ships found port here during the Civil War."

"I had no idea this place had that kind of history," she said.

He nodded. "I'm a bit of a history buff, especially when it comes to the military."

"I suppose that can come in handy when you're a Navy SEAL. After all, those who forget history are doomed to repeat it."

"Very good. George Santayana, Spanish poet and philosopher."

"I didn't actually know who said it, only that the words were true."

He pointed to the harbor. "Most people don't realize the significance of a harbor, especially a deep water one like this. It offers anchorage and safety to ships in need. Especially in times of war, that's important. The crew needs fuel and food and a place to rest. It's vital to have that safe place to refresh before heading back out into the storms."

"We all need that, don't we?" Bree's gaze fluttered toward Dez, and a smile brushed her lips.

"Yes, we do."

Bree shifted, her thoughts turning things over. "So, I walked in on Griff earlier, and he was looking at a photo. He looked like he'd been caught doing something he shouldn't. It was weird."

"It was probably his daughter."

"I didn't know he had a child."

Dez nodded. "A little girl named Ada. She's three and totally adorable. Griff . . . he still has a hard time being away from her, though he doesn't talk about it much."

"I can't imagine . . ." Before they could talk anymore, she grabbed Dez's arm. "You see those two guys?"

He followed her gaze across the harbor where two men docked a boat.

"They look like . . . Trixie's brothers."

CHAPTER SEVENTEEN

BREE FROZE before nodding at the two men in the distance. They climbed from a boat and started toward an old truck parked near the dock.

"What are Trixie's brothers doing here?" Bree muttered. "We should call the police chief and let her know."

"I think that's a good idea."

Dez grabbed his phone and dialed the chief's number. With the phone on speaker, he told her that the Dare brothers had been spotted.

"That's good to know," Chief Chambers said. "I just talked to two witnesses who saw them harassing Kyle Thompson before he was found dead. Right now, they're our top suspects."

"They're here at the harbor right now, and they

appear to be walking toward their vehicle." Dez didn't take his eyes off the men.

"See if you can stall them," Chief Chambers said. "Don't do anything that would put you in danger. But if you can slow them down, I'm on my way there right now with an arrest warrant in hand."

"I'll see what I can do," Dez said.

Bree had heard the chief's request, but the very thought of it caused more fear to shimmy up her spine.

"Maybe you should stay away," she said. "If these guys are the ones who opened fire at my concert, they're not someone you should mess with."

"I like to think I can handle myself."

"I'm sure you can. But when it comes to gun fights, it's all a matter of who is the quickest draw as much as the best aim."

Dez glanced at her and gave her a look. Bree couldn't quite read it. Was he annoyed by the suggestion that he wasn't invulnerable?

Bree wasn't sure. She just didn't want to see this bad situation get even worse. Too many people had already been hurt.

As the two men started to climb into their truck, Dez put his own vehicle in Park and reached for the door handle.

"Stay here," he said. "And lock the doors."

"Dez . . ." Bree heard the worry in her voice. There was so much on the line here.

"I'll be smart. I promise."

She stared at him another moment and nodded. It was strange how she had only known him a couple of days, yet she already felt like she'd known him months.

He felt more like a friend than he did a bodyguard, for that matter. He was the kind of friend that everybody could use—a good listener, protective, yet, at the same time, fun to be around.

Where exactly were Bree's thoughts going with this? She wasn't sure. All those realizations seemed to come out of the blue.

She was not attracted to Dez Rodriguez. That was one thing she knew for sure.

Yet another part of her knew she wasn't being honest with herself. Any hot-blooded woman would be attracted to Dez Rodriguez. In fact, every woman they had passed when she was with Dez had their eyes on the man. He was just that type of person.

Anxiety bubbled through her as she watched him stride toward the truck in the distance.

She squeezed her eyes shut and prayed for a

good outcome. But, despite her prayer, worry still churned in her stomach.

DEZ HAD his gun tucked safely in a holster at his waistband beneath his shirt, just in case he needed it. But he hoped it didn't come down to that.

He needed to think of a safe way to stop these guys until Cassidy could arrive.

Just as the driver was about to close his door, Dez waved his hand in the air and yelled, "Wait!"

The driver froze before rising from his seat.

Dez took a good look at him. The man was probably in his early thirties. He had a dark, bushy beard and wore waders with a heavy, waterproof jacket.

He definitely looked like the stereotypical fisherman.

But was he just a fisherman? Or was this man also a killer?

Dez had been face-to-face with vile people before, and certainly he could handle himself with this guy.

"I'm trying to find Goodwin's Charters." Dez strode toward them. "Do you have any idea where they are? I've driven up and down this marina three times now, and I still haven't seen any signs."

"No, man," the driver said. "I'm not from around here. Sorry. Can't help."

"You catch anything out there today?"

A look of annoyance crossed the man's face. He had started to sit back down but he froze again, as if he'd changed his mind about brushing off Dez. "Got a few things. Sometimes it's just about being in the right place at the right time to get a good catch, though."

"I know that's true. Did you guys use a charter? Just in case I can't find this guy, I might need to look for someone else." He kept his motions casual, chatty.

Now the look of annoyance was full-blown. This guy did not want to have a conversation with him. That was too bad.

"Come on, Landon," the other brother called, motioning for him to get back in the truck. "We need to go."

"We rented a boat. I don't need a captain or crew. I just need a boat and fishing line. Now, if you'll excuse me . . . we have other things we need to do." He nodded toward his brother.

Dez paused in front of the truck. He wasn't sure

how much longer he could keep up this charade before they decided just to take off.

"I am also looking for a good place to eat around here," Dez continued. "Know of any places?"

Landon shook his head. "Look, man, if you want answers to all these questions, find a tour guide. Look online. Stop asking us."

Dez raised his hands. "Sorry, sorry. You guys just looked approachable. Like the kind of guys who might want to help another guy out. I'm with my girl." Dez nodded toward the car where Bree sat. The windows were tinted, so he knew the man wouldn't recognize her, only see her outline.

"I wish we could help. Sorry, bro. We've got to go."

Dez had one more trick up his sleeve. "Hey, did I see you guys at that Trixie Dare concert?"

The two brothers looked at each other, as if he'd sounded suspicious.

"Yeah, we were there," Landon said. "Trixie is our sister."

Dez's features went slack, as if impressed. "Is she? That's awesome. You two are practically celebrities then. You have a very talented sister."

"We think so too. She should have a lot more accolades than she does." Landon scowled.

"She should have a lot more accolades than that fake Bree Jordan." Dez hated to say the words, but he had to play a role here.

Now he had the brothers' full attention.

"Exactly," Landon said. "Bree doesn't even write her own music. She basically is just a voice. She has people who tell her what to wear, how to act, how to sing. Trixie, on the other hand . . . she's the real thing."

Dez was careful to conceal his true feelings. "It looks like somebody else shared your thoughts. Maybe that's why they tried to take Bree out at that concert." He let out a disbelieving chuckle.

"Yeah, I don't know anything about that." Landon gripped the truck door, as if ready to climb in again.

Come on, Cassidy. Where are you?

"Are you sure about that?" Dez asked.

Landon stepped from behind his door and slammed it. His body seemed to puff up with anger as he took a step closer to Dez. "Who are you really?"

"Can't I just be a tourist asking questions?" Dez shrugged.

"You could be, but you're not. Now what are you doing here?"

Dez knew his charade was over. "I'm trying to figure out who shot at Bree Jordan."

The man's eyebrows rose. "Do you think it was us?"

"I think it's a possibility."

"Then you need to recheck your possibilities because you are barking up the wrong tree." Landon stepped closer, almost as if challenging Dez to a fight.

Dez wasn't going to take the bait. That wasn't who he was anymore. Maybe in high school, but he had come a long way since then.

"I heard you were out on the water during Bree's concert," Dez prodded.

"Yeah. So? What's it to you? Can't two guys go out fishing?"

"Did you have a gun with you?" As Dez asked the question, his gaze drifted to Landon's waistband. He saw the weapon there.

Cassidy needed to get here before this turned ugly. Dez didn't want to take matters into his own hands—not any more than he already had, at least.

"Whether or not I have a gun is none of your business. And I'm done with this conversation." Landon reached for the truck door again.

"I don't think you should go yet," Dez said.

"And why is that?"

Just as the question left his mouth, Dez heard the sirens in the distance. Landon jumped in the truck and threw it into Drive. They took off toward the exit of the harbor area.

He prayed they didn't get away.

CHAPTER EIGHTEEN

WITH TRIXIE'S brothers behind bars, Bree felt like she could breathe a lot easier. Maybe going to this engagement party tonight wouldn't be a big deal after all. It would give her the chance to get out, since most of the danger had passed.

From what she understood, Chief Chambers had found photos of her at the beach house where the Dare brothers were staying. They also had guns with them, the same kind that were used in the shooting. That, when combined with the confrontation someone saw between the brothers and Kyle, seemed to cement the fact that they were most likely behind the shooting and Kyle's murder.

Chief Chambers had made the arrest, and the

North Carolina State Bureau of Investigation was also there to question the men.

At six o'clock, Dez and Bree left to go to the party. Apparently, it was going to be held at Chief Chambers' place. From what Dez had told her, it was also the temporary headquarters for Blackout.

Bree knew that it was strange, but she felt weirdly excited to be doing something that felt so normal. Nothing had felt normal in her life for a long time.

They pulled up to a cottage by the ocean. She thought it was charming. Six little colorful cabanas lined the outside of the property, each with a hammock strung on the porch.

A traditional beach cottage with weathered cedar shingles and dormers stood as the centerpiece of the property. It had a cozy second story and a screened-in porch that faced the ocean.

Bree's place was admirable, but this place could be featured in a painting.

"This is where I stay when I'm not bodyguarding." Dez nodded toward the pink cabana.

"Pink fits you," she teased.

He chuckled. "I'm man enough to embrace it."

Yes, he was. He was all man with his confidence and muscles. "Was all of this built just for Blackout?"

"Ty actually built it for a retreat center he started called Hope House. But when he doesn't need to use the cabanas for that event, we are allowed to use them."

"And where do you stay when the retreats are in session?"

"Ty's parents have a cottage right next door. During this last session, we all moved over there since they went to Florida for the winter. But we are looking for a more permanent solution. However, all land on this island is pretty expensive. We're trying to raise the capital that we need."

"I hope you're able to do that."

"So are we." Dez parked the car, and they climbed out. At least six vehicles were already there.

Dez had told her that, just to be safe, he and his guys would keep a lookout on the perimeter of the area. They couldn't afford to let down their guard . . . not yet, at least.

As soon as they crossed the sand dune onto the beach, Bree saw the crowd in the distance. The party looked like something right out of one of the songs she'd written.

A bonfire blazed on the beach and tiki torches had been set up along the perimeter. Several picnic tables had been pushed together, and food stretched across them. A man played the guitar while everyone else talked and laughed together.

Bree could hardly pull her eyes away. "This is . . . perfect."

Dez nodded. "Yeah, it pretty much is, isn't it? I've done a lot of things in my thirty-two years. And, at the end of it all, I realize that it's the people you're around who make life worth living. That it's the moments like this."

Bree smiled at him. "If you have people who have your back and you have theirs, then I would say you have a lot in this life."

As she said the words, Bree realized that it wasn't something that she could say for herself. In fact, she couldn't name one single person who she felt loved her unconditionally.

That thought caused a burst of sadness to fill her.

DEZ INTRODUCED Bree to everybody at the party, but there was no chance she would remember all their names.

She'd met Ty, Cassidy's husband. He was also a

former Navy SEAL, and he had a boy next door turned strong, strapping man vibe to him.

Griff was there, being his normal aloof self.

She met Colton Locke again, the fearless leader of the team. Colton's girlfriend, Elise Oliver, stood beside him, clearly his opposite with her petite features and gentle smile.

She also met Benjamin James, the fourth and final member of the team, and the youngest.

Lisa Dillinger from The Crazy Chefette, and her husband, Braden, were there. Lisa had brought several side dishes, and Bree couldn't wait to try each one.

The list of attendees continued.

Wes O'Neill, who ran a kayak tour company, and his girlfriend, Paige Henderson. Bree recognized Paige from the police station. She worked the front desk there.

Jack Wilson, a pastor, and his wife, Juliet.

Mac MacArthur, the former police chief here in Lantern Beach and current mayor.

Two of the final people she met were the guests of honor, Austin Brooks and Skye Lavinia.

"Congratulations, you two." Bree tapped into her Southern roots and pulled the two of them into a congratulatory hug. Austin, with his dark hair, and scruffy beard, and Skye, with her bohemian style and long hair, seemed like a perfect couple.

As Skye pulled away, her eyes remained on Bree. "I have to admit, I'm a little starstruck right now. I love your music. The songs are just so upbeat, and they make me happy."

"And anything that makes her happy makes me happy," Austin said.

"Sounds like you have figured out the recipe for a good marriage then." Bree flashed a smile.

The two of them exchanged a glance and grinned.

"No, really," Bree said. "Congratulations. When's the big day?"

"This weekend," Skye said. "We're not doing anything big. Just a ceremony on the beach. That's all we need."

"We told each other as soon as we finished flipping a house, we would get married," Austin said. "Unfortunately, the house took much longer than we anticipated."

"But at least that gave us some time to save up money," Skye said.

"Anyway." Austin took a step back. "Enough about us. Welcome to our party. Grab some food and have a good time."

Bree glanced back at Dez and saw him surveying the area. He was more nervous than he wanted to appear, wasn't he?

As much as Bree would like to think that today was normal, Bree needed to remind herself that it wasn't. These people weren't her friends. This island wasn't her home. And Dez was nothing more than a bodyguard.

If she was smart, Bree would push those things to the forefront of her mind and make sure they remained there.

CHAPTER NINETEEN

DEZ COULDN'T SEEM to take his eyes off Bree. She had that effect on people. It was part of the reason she was so good at what she did—she had charisma. When she smiled, she lit up the room. When she talked, people listened. And when she sang . . . everything else disappeared.

At least, for most people it did—not including her manager or people who wanted to make a profit off her. Those people seemed to only act like they were concerned about her as a person, when they were actually mostly concerned about their bank accounts.

Dez felt his muscles tense at the thought of it. His thoughts went back to the Savages, the deadly terrorists he'd fought on his last mission. So many of their actions were born out of the desire for money and power. That, when fueled with a hatred for freedom-loving countries, had created a dangerous mix.

He supposed those deadly attitudes weren't just reserved for wars overseas, though. Even in biblical times, it was warned, "For the love of money is a root of all kinds of evil."

The party had been fun, filled with lots of food and laughter. But now it was starting to settle down, and they had all laid out blankets by the bonfire to sit around and talk.

This was one of Dez's favorite things to do since he'd moved to Lantern Beach. There was something about sitting by the ocean with a fire that was so serene it made his soul feel at peace.

And peace was not something that should ever be discounted.

"So, Cassidy, any updates on that property where Gilead's Cove was located?" Griff asked.

"It's still caught up in that lawsuit right now," Cassidy said. "But that hasn't changed any of the tension surrounding the area. People still have very strong feelings."

"It would've been nice to have a hotel when the festival was going on here this week," Austin said.

"Which isn't to say that I am in favor of the hotel itself."

"I don't disagree that there would be advantages to it." Cassidy pulled a blanket around her shoulders. "However, I'm trying to stay impartial."

"Speaking of advantages to the festival, how was business this week at The Crazy Chefette?" Wes asked. "I know you were afraid you'd be bombarded."

"It would've been fine, if Lisa hadn't been feeling sick lately," Braden said.

As soon as the words left his mouth, Lisa nudged him.

It was too late. Everyone in the group had their eyes on the couple.

"Is everything okay?" Concern laced Cassidy's voice.

Lisa gave Braden another look. "Everything is fine. I'm just feeling a little under the weather."

"Hey, you're not cooking our food while sick, are you?" Wes asked. "Because I've eaten there twice this week."

"Don't worry, it's not contagious," Lisa insisted, casting another look at her husband.

Everyone continued to stare, wondering exactly what she was getting at.

Finally, she let out a sigh. "I didn't want to say anything here because this is Austin and Skye's big day. But Braden and I ... we're expecting."

A round of congratulations and hugs went around the circle.

Though Dez hadn't been on the island long, Ty's friends had become his friends. And he was happy for them.

Part of him felt a touch of jealousy. As he saw his friends pairing off around him, he realized what was missing from his own life. He liked to pretend that he was happy being single and going out on dates with various women and never committing. But he would give anything to settle down, to find the woman of his dreams, to have a couple of kids. Or three. Maybe even four. He didn't know.

He'd had such a happy childhood himself. He wanted what his mom and dad had for his own future.

As the thought entered his mind, Dez suddenly felt keenly aware of Bree beside him. What did she want for her future? Was she content just to travel and do this for the rest of her life?

It didn't matter. It was out of the question. *She* was out of the question. Bree was famous and not the type to probably want to settle down. How could she? She was on the road too much.

And Bree was his client. Dez needed to keep that in mind. Even if there was a connection between them, Bree was off-limits. There was no dating on the job, as Griff had gleefully reminded him.

Besides, Leah . . .

Every time he started to get close to someone, her picture flashed in his mind, followed by bad memories of his heartache.

Was love worth the risk? He used to say no. But since he'd met Bree . . .

He shoved the thoughts aside.

A few minutes later, Ty pulled out his guitar again. He strummed some before glancing over at Bree.

"Would you mind playing something for us?" he asked. "I'm just an amateur over here, playing stuff that I picked up on VideoStream."

"I think you're doing a great job." Bree smiled softly, her face illuminated by the dancing flames of the bonfire.

"We'd love to hear you play something," Cassidy said. "No pressure, but . . . we're all fans."

After a moment of hesitation, Bree took the guitar and began to strum it.

"Anyone here sing baritone?"

"Dez has a really nice voice," Griff said with a grin.

The man was such an instigator.

"Take that back," Dez said. "I do not."

"Oh, I've heard him singing in the shower," Colton said. "He does have a set of lungs on him."

"Thanks a lot, guys," Dez muttered. He could always count on his friends.

"He has a lot of hidden superpowers," Benjamin said.

Bree glanced at him, curiosity flickering in her gaze. "Like what?"

"He can make anyone want to fall in love with him," Griff said. "I've always thought if he were to combine that ability with his singing talent, he would pretty much conquer the world."

A bunch of good-natured chuckling went around the circle at the ribbing.

Dez just shook his head. He wanted to deny it, but he knew if he did, they'd only continue to give him a hard time. It was best to take these things in stride.

"Okay, okay," he finally said. "I do like to sing sometimes. There. I admit the truth."

"Great," Bree said. "Because I'm going to need

some help on the chorus of this song. I know you'll pick up on it pretty easily."

She began strumming one of her hit songs. Except, instead of singing it at the pop tempo everyone was used to hearing it, she did her own version of it—a more acoustic, folksy style.

When they got to the chorus, Dez hesitated a minute before joining in. Their voices blended together surprisingly well.

When they finished, everyone around them applauded.

"You two should take this show on the road," Colton said. "Except that I might lose one of my best guys."

"Hey, what am I? Chopped liver?" Griff asked.

"And me?" Benjamin piped in.

"You're all my best guys," Colton said. "That's why I asked you to join me here, of course."

"Good recovery," Elise said, giving Colton a knowing look before resting her head on his shoulder. He wrapped an arm around her and kissed the top of her head.

As Dez and Bree exchanged a smile, he felt something pass between them. Something unexpected. Something he hadn't felt in a long time.

So far, this evening had felt perfect.

It was too bad that it was going to have to end and reality would kick in again.

Bree Jordan was off-limits, he reminded himself. He had to keep his distance.

***

BREE PLAYED A COUPLE MORE SONGS. Except, instead of doing the versions that people were used to hearing, she put her own spin on them. It wasn't often she shared these versions with anybody. Mostly because people didn't want to hear these versions.

Not people, exactly. More like Emerson.

She did a couple of her originals, as well as a few covers that people knew and could sing along with.

The whole evening had been fun.

But her favorite part had been when Dez sang with her. His friends weren't lying when they said he had a good voice. It was smooth and pleasant, and when their two voices mingled together . . . it was like the two of them should go on the road together.

Not that she ever saw Dez actually wanting to do that. But it had been fun to let their voices blend into one. When that happened—which was rare—it almost felt magical.

That had happened tonight with Dez, and, as a result, her entire insides felt like they had been candy-coated with something warm and gooey.

It was a feeling Bree hadn't felt in a very long time.

She craved connection more than she realized. It was more than just about music. It was about finding someone she fit with.

When the fire started dwindling, it seemed to signal it was time to leave.

As Bree said goodbye to everybody, Skye caught her arm. "Are you still going to be around this weekend?"

Bree thought about it for a moment. "There's a good chance that I will be."

"If you are, and I know this is really forward of me to ask this, but I would love it if you could sing that song at my wedding."

Surprise washed through her. "Which song?"

"I don't know. I've never heard it before. But it was the one about love being like the ocean on a cloudless, beautiful day. It was just haunting. Where did you get that song?"

"I wrote it." A burst of satisfaction flooded her.

"Why isn't it on one of your albums?"

Bree shrugged, knowing better than to go into all the details. "It didn't make the cut, unfortunately."

"Well, I love it. I think it's one of your best."

Bree smiled at the encouragement. "I would be honored to sing that at your wedding."

Skye squealed and threw her arms around her. "Thank you! That just makes my whole week."

"I thought our wedding made your whole week," Austin teased.

"I mean . . . it does. Pretend you didn't hear that." Skye flashed another grin at Bree. "Okay, I'll be in touch."

Several minutes later, Dez and Bree climbed back into his borrowed car to start back to her house for the evening. She almost felt sad to return to her normal, everyday life. Tonight had been so refreshing.

"I'd say you were a hit tonight," Dez said.

"Me? How about you and your hidden talents . . . ?"

"I just like to sing for fun."

"Well, you did a good job with it."

"Thank you. I appreciate that. But I think I'll stick to being a bodyguard."

"You do a good job with that also. But if you want

to be a singing bodyguard, you might put a whole new spin on the profession."

He chuckled. "Yes, I'd say that I would."

As they started down the road, Bree saw Dez's shoulders tighten and knew something was wrong. He glanced in the rearview mirror.

"What is it?" she asked, all her laid-back vibes disappearing.

"I think someone is following us. Brace yourself because I don't know what's going to happen next."

CHAPTER TWENTY

DEZ GLANCED in the rearview mirror again and saw the headlights moving closer. His gut told him that somebody was following them.

Was it the same person who'd killed Kyle and tried to shoot Bree? It seemed likely. What if the Dare brothers weren't behind this after all?

He pressed on the accelerator as they headed down the road.

"Call Cassidy," he told Bree. "Tell her what's going on. We might need backup now."

Bree nodded, her hands shaky as she pulled the phone from her pocket. "I'm on it."

Dez rattled off Cassidy's number before looking into the rearview mirror again. The lights were practically right on him now, so close that he almost couldn't see them. He needed to think of a way to lose this guy while not hurting anyone else in the process.

His thoughts shifted, and he pictured the layout of the island, its roads. One main highway cut through the middle of the island, stretching from north to south. Several side roads branched out from it, most of them dead ends.

There was only one solution he could think of. He hoped he could make it to the area he needed to get to in order to put his plan into action.

He hit the accelerator harder and heard Bree gasp beside him. Spontaneously, he reached over and squeezed her hand.

"Trust me," he said.

She squeezed his hand back, a little harder than he expected as she pressed her eyes shut. "I'm trying."

He released his grip and put both hands back on the steering wheel. He'd gained a little space between his car and the one behind him. But he knew it was only a matter of time before that vehicle caught up with them.

Only one more mile by his estimations. If they could make it that far, Dez could put an end to this chase. And, if he could figure out who was in the car, maybe he could put an end to this whole ordeal.

Finally, Dez saw the area he'd been trying to reach.

This was it. The moment he would see if his plan worked or not. He only hoped his memory wasn't faulty.

He was headed toward the lighthouse on the south end of the island. Right before the landmark, the area was surrounded by woods.

Just as he reached a bend in the dark road, he jerked the steering wheel to the left. His car swerved around, doing a donut on the street.

The driver behind him hadn't anticipated the turn. The vehicle swerved before crashing into one of the trees near the bend. The sickly sound of crushed metal filled the air, followed by the smell of smoke.

Dez threw the car in Park and reached for the door.

"Stay here," he ordered. "I'm about to find out who has been behind this."

BREE WATCHED out the window while simultaneously lifting prayers. Whoever was behind that steering wheel could be dangerous. Most likely he *was* dangerous. And Dez was headed right toward him.

Images tried to claim her. Images of Dez being shot or hurt. She squeezed her eyes shut, unable to deal with those pictures. Dez fascinated her. There was still so much about him that she wanted to get to know.

All that could change if the wrong person climbed from the driver's seat.

She opened her eyes again but held her breath now. Was the driver okay? It was hard to see anything. The windshield was smashed. The hood crumpled. Smoke poured from the engine.

She watched as Dez jerked open the driver side door. He reached into the vehicle. A moment later, he pulled somebody from the car.

Bree's eyes widened. Was that . . . what?

It was.

Trixie Dare.

Without hesitation, Bree opened her door and stormed over to the scene. She wanted to hear what this woman had to say.

"It's your fault!" Trixie screamed at Bree. Blood drizzled from her nose. Glass looked like glitter in her hair and on her jacket. A cut lined the side of her forehead.

Trixie didn't seem to care—or notice.

"What are you talking about?" Bree was thankful that Dez still held the woman's arms because Trixie looked ready to pounce at the first opportunity.

Bree's only comfort were the sirens she heard in the distance coming their way.

"You got my brothers arrested. All because you're angry at me for those accusations I leveled against your songwriter."

"That's not true. The police chief asked me for a list of people who had grudges against me. Your name came up. I never accused you of doing this, though."

"I might not like you," Trixie growled. "But that doesn't mean I would go this far."

"You just tried to run us off the road." Dez held the woman's arms behind her. "You're not making a very good case for yourself."

"I just wanted to talk."

"We're talking now," Bree said. "What else did you want to say?"

"You don't deserve everything you have," Trixie said, venom shooting from her eyes.

"And let me guess? You do?" Bree wasn't challenging her. Instead, she felt exhausted. She somehow knew Trixie wouldn't listen to her, no matter what she said.

"I've worked my butt off, and then someone as talentless as you comes in and takes everything from me."

"The fame was never yours to take," Bree said. "And I never saw you as my competition. I saw you as a fellow singer. At one point, I even suggested that maybe we could travel together and you could be my opening act."

Trixie spat on the ground. "Like I would ever want to open for you."

Bree shook her head and took a step back. She was wasting her breath. "I can see now that this was a bad idea. But I never had it out for you, Trixie. I would love to see you succeed. And, believe me, every day I feel like I don't deserve to be where I am. I don't know why things happened as they did, and I ended up in the spotlight while you didn't. But, looking at you now, I'm inclined to think that you weren't ready for it."

As Trixie muttered more things at Bree, Bree walked back to the car. As she reached her door, Chief Chambers and her crew pulled up.

A few minutes later, they had Trixie in custody.

CHAPTER TWENTY-ONE

"DO you want to talk about it?" Dez asked as they headed back to Bree's place. He knew that all of this had to be taking a toll on her.

Bree swallowed hard, her gaze appearing unsettled as she stared out the window. "You've gotten a crash course in the entertainment industry, haven't you?"

"Are things always like this?"

"No, not really. But money makes people do strange things sometimes. So does fame. My mom used to read me a verse in the Bible that talked about it being easier for a camel to go through the eye of a needle than a rich man to enter heaven. I didn't know what that meant at first, but now I see it.

There's just so much corruption. Whenever money and fame are involved, there seems to be a scandal."

The fact that she was aware of that seemed like a good thing. "I thought you handled the situation well. I think you've handled *all* of this well."

"That's good to know because I feel like I'm breaking into pieces on the inside." Her voice cracked.

Dez squeezed her shoulder. "It would be a lot for anyone to handle. Not only do you have a killer coming after you, but you have a manager who could be Satan's righthand man and a competing singer with blood in her eyes."

Bree rubbed her forehead, almost as if she had a headache coming on. "It has been a lot. Maybe a little sleep will make me feel better. Then, again, tomorrow's a new day. I can't help but wonder what problems it might bring."

"Let tomorrow worry about itself," Dez said.

She offered a fleeting smile. "Great advice. And I will. But when we get back to the house, I do need to make a couple of phone calls. There's something I want to look into."

She had something else on her mind, didn't she? Dez couldn't imagine what it might be. But he did know her problems weren't over yet.

ONCE BREE WAS BACK at the house and tucked safely into her bedroom, she picked up her phone and called Carson Black. Though it was past midnight, she knew Carson well enough to know she would still be awake. Like a lot of people in the entertainment business, staying up late was an industry standard.

Carson answered on the second ring. "Is this the one and only Bree Jordan?"

"It's me," Bree said, smiling at the dramatic tone of her friend's voice. "Sorry to be calling so late. But I have a couple of questions, and you're the only person I know who might be able to help me. Is this a bad time?"

"I've always got time for you."

Bree could hear Carson moving. The music and chatter in the background disappeared, and quiet filled the line. Bree sat down on the edge of her bed and stared at the stark darkness out her window. She wished she could be fascinated by the world outside instead of terrified.

"I'm so sorry about what happened at your concert," Carson said.

"I appreciate your concern. We're all holding on.

I'm grateful that everyone is still alive." She pulled a pillow onto her lap and squeezed it.

"We all are. If there's anything you need, you just let us know. The whole community is there for you."

"There actually *is* something I need," Bree started.

Carson Black was another of Emerson's prodigies. She'd been discovered about five years before Bree. At the height of her success, she'd had five number one hit singles and sold out her tours. However, like many in the industry, her fame had quickly worn off and she'd been replaced with newer, younger models. Today, she had taken a side gig hosting a reality music competition on TV. The change seemed to fit Carson, however.

Bree wouldn't call Carson a good friend, but they had spoken several times at different events where they'd been together. Carson had always told her if she ever needed anything, to give her a call. And that's exactly what Bree was doing right now.

"The question is about Emerson," Bree started.

Even though Carson didn't say anything immediately, Bree could sense a change in atmosphere of the conversation. Carson's voice sounded stiff as she asked, "What do you need to know?"

"I was talking to Lloyd today when his girlfriend,

Jill, came in. She claims that Emerson has written all of the contracts with his singers in such a way that he gets the majority of their money. I also heard that he sadly underpays bands and other staff members that he hires."

Carson was quiet again for another moment. Bree braced herself for whatever Carson had to say. Would Carson rebuke her? Or confirm Bree's suspicions?

"It's true," Carson said. "The way Emerson words the contracts is crazy. I even had three lawyers look at mine before I signed with him, but some things still got by. It doesn't help that he's your manager, producer, and that he's in charge of finances. He's managed to get a cut for himself in all those things. I know it seems like you're making a lot now, but, in the long run, there's a good chance that you won't be."

Bree swallowed hard, a feeling of dread already forming in her stomach. "Is that right? Why didn't you tell me that before?"

"I started to," she said. "Do you remember when we were at that concert in Nashville together? It was on the Fourth of July, and it was only the second or third time that we'd met. You were so excited to be working with Emerson."

Bree remembered that day well. It was like the honeymoon period of her career, and she'd kept pinching herself, not believing this was all real. "Yes, I do."

"I started to tell you to be careful, but you started chattering on and on about what a great opportunity this was. You even said that it wasn't about money or fame, but about pursuing your art and passion. I could see it in your eyes, that excitement. I didn't want to burst your bubble. Besides, if you meant it when you said you didn't care about money and fame, I figured everything would be okay."

"Money and fame have never been my goal. I just wanted to reach people with my songs. But I haven't even been able to perform any of my own songs. They got buried, and I have very little creative control over what I do."

Carson sighed. "That's something else that Emerson does really well. He's a manipulator. He knows how to make you feel silly when you suggest things that he doesn't agree with. Granted, he does have experience that speaks for itself."

Bree stared out the window. "Do you think he's shady?"

Carson remained quiet for a minute. "Like I said, Emerson presents himself in a way that takes any suspicion off of him. But, when you strip all that away, then I have to say yes. It's why I cut ties with him and went out on my own. To this day, he hates me."

"Are you the only one he's done this to?"

Carson snorted. "No, he has a whole line of people he's done this to. He's a snake. He may be a brilliant snake, but he is still a snake. And, by the way, I've heard rumors that he pays people off with gag orders if they figure out what he's doing."

"What can I do?" A sick feeling gurgled in her stomach.

"When is your contract up?"

"In two years."

"Then in two years, you don't sign up with him again. Until then, you have to grin and bear it. I wish I had better news for you, but I don't. I'm sorry."

As Bree ended the call, her head pounded.

She needed to talk to Emerson. And she would, first thing in the morning. She would go to his place. She wanted to hear exactly what he had to say.

Coming to Lantern Beach had proven to be a wakeup call in so many ways.

CHAPTER TWENTY-TWO

DEZ DIDN'T EXPECT to feel the burst of pleasure he did when he spotted Bree coming into the kitchen the next morning. When he had gone to bed last night, he'd felt both happier and more concerned than he had in a long time.

He wanted to be in denial about why he felt so happy, but he knew the truth. He was enjoying his time with Bree way too much. He hadn't felt this way . . . since Leah, he supposed.

Leah had shattered his heart into so many pieces that it hadn't been the same since. If Dez was smart, he would stay away from Bree now and try to put the brakes on any of these feelings. Nothing good could come from him pining after a popstar.

Soon, Bree would be leaving this island and

returning to her regularly scheduled life. To ask her to do anything but that would be a disservice to her dreams and to everyone who loved her music.

That's why Dez needed to keep his focus on keeping her safe. It was the best bet all around.

He studied her for a moment from his place at the breakfast bar. She was already dressed, with her hair fixed and makeup on. He didn't know what she planned to do today, but she was obviously ready for it.

He stood and grabbed an empty coffee cup. "Would you like some?"

"I would love some." She offered a grateful smile.

He fixed the drink for her, just as Bree liked it, and handed the cup to her. The two of them sat at the breakfast bar together.

"I'd never been to Lantern Beach before this concert," she started. "But I heard about the invitation and then did my research. I knew I had to come. This place reminded me of my family vacations when I was a child. We always went to Pawleys Island."

"Are you from South Carolina?"

She nodded. "I am. A little town outside of Charleston. That's where my family still lives."

"What do your parents do for a living?"

"My dad is a teacher, and my mom stayed home with the kids. We were very close . . . until I broke tradition by not listening to them."

"Do you ever try to call them?"

She took a long sip of coffee before answering. "I did at first. But they never took my calls. Once I called from a number my mom didn't recognize. She answered. But when she heard my voice, she hung up."

"Ouch."

"Yes, ouch."

"Has the sacrifice been worth it?"

Bree glanced at him, the question lingering in her gaze for a minute. "I don't know. I wish there was no either-or situation."

A few minutes of silence fell.

Dez glanced at her. Bree seemed preoccupied as she stared outside, a far-off look in her eyes. He'd figured she might feel lighter today, like some of her problems were disappearing since Trixie and her brothers were in jail. Apparently not.

"You look like you have something on your mind," he started.

She looked at him, still not smiling. "I do. I talked to Carson Black last night, and it turns out that Emerson has taken a lot of the artists he developed to the bank. I feel so foolish, to be honest."

A surge of anger went up Dez's spine. He knew that man was nothing but trouble. "There's nothing to feel foolish about. It seems like he may be in the habit of taking advantage of people who want to make a career in music."

She gripped her coffee mug. "I should've known better. But with my parents closing me out of their lives, I didn't have money for a lawyer. I did talk to a few people about the contract before I signed it, but they weren't people in the industry. All my friends told me to go for it. They knew the stars that Emerson had developed, and it seemed like I would be a fool if I didn't take this opportunity."

"It was the chance of a lifetime."

"It's not that I think that I deserve to get all the money from record sales and concerts. Not at all. But I also don't think I should be taken advantage of."

If there was one thing Dez had learned about Bree in the brief amount of time he'd known her, it was that she wasn't the materialistic, fame-seeking star he'd assumed she would be. She was just a woman trying to make a living doing what she loved.

"No one could fault you for that," he said.

Bree's gaze met his. "I need to go talk to Emerson."

"When? Right now?"

She nodded slowly, almost solemnly. "Yes, right now. I don't want to give him a heads up. Because I know that will just give him time to make up more excuses. I want to see his face when I confront him."

"If that's what you want to do, I'll be there."

She took a sip of her coffee, her gaze distant again until her eyes met his. Finally, the first hint of a smile tugged at her lips. "Thank you."

"No problem. At your service."

Her smile slowly disappeared.

Dez had picked his words on purpose—to remind himself of his professional boundaries.

But Bree felt something more also, didn't she? Why did that both delight and concern him?

Bree cleared her throat. "Are there any updates on the case? Have you talked to Chief Chambers?"

"I talked to her this morning briefly, but I didn't hear anything new."

"At least, Trixie and her brothers are behind bars. As much as I hate to see someone so talented get caught up in something like this, in any case, I can breathe a little easier." She paused. "I suppose now that they've been arrested, I may not need a bodyguard."

Dez felt the lump in his throat. He knew it was ridiculous, but he didn't like the thought of being away from her. They were just now getting to know each other, and it seemed a shame to cut things off just as they'd started.

"Maybe not," Dez finally said.

"I should probably keep you around for just a little while longer until we hear something for sure." She shrugged and part of her lip started to curl into a smile.

Dez shrugged also. "Probably a good idea. Just to be sure."

Their gazes met for a minute, and something passed between them. An understanding of sorts. Whatever it was, Dez wanted to know more.

As he shifted, his hand hit his coffee mug and liquid poured across the table.

They both jumped to their feet, the moment over.

"I'll grab some paper towels," Bree said, scurrying away.

What was with him becoming a klutz around Bree?

So much for being Mr. Charming and Smooth.

BREE FELT the anxiety rise in her as they traveled down the road thirty minutes later. Emerson's house wasn't far away, and she was certain this was what she wanted to do. But that didn't stop her nerves from materializing.

She knew Emerson wouldn't react well to the conversation. But she'd already called a lawyer this morning and asked him to look over her contract. She had emailed it to him. She knew it would take time for him to review all of the fine print there, however.

Something about knowing that Dez was going to be with her brought Bree a surge of courage and comfort. There was something about him that was very reassuring to her.

Part of Bree wanted to revel in giddiness at the thought of Dez. Not only was he handsome, but she felt like the two of them had a unique connection. Did he feel it too? Or was it just her?

She might ask. But then, again, what was the point? Her home base was in LA. His was on the other side of the country on an island accessible only by ferry.

A relationship between them ... if Dez was even interested ... would be challenging, at best.

Before they reached Emerson's house, Bree's phone rang. It was her financial manager. She'd also placed a call to him last night.

"Hey, Bill," she answered. "I wanted to talk to you about setting up a fund to help pay for the medical expenses of the shooting victims."

"That's a great idea, Bree," he said. "But ... I don't think you can do that."

"What do you mean?" Her spine stiffened.

"I just checked the account. You haven't been paid in months."

She sucked in a breath. "What do you mean, I haven't been paid in months?"

Dez glanced over at her, his eyebrows shoved together.

"I don't know how it slipped past me," Bill said. "I'm usually more on top of things like this. But the last time you got paid was in October. I tried to call Emerson before I called you, so I could talk to him about it. He didn't answer. I'm going to keep on digging into this."

"Thanks, Bill." As Bree ended the call, a bad feeling lingered in her stomach.

"Emerson hasn't been paying you?" Dez asked.

She shook her head. "No, he hasn't. I . . . I don't know what to think. I've been on the road, where all my expenses are taken care of. I haven't even thought about following up to see if my paycheck was coming in."

"He's dirty," Dez muttered.

"I think you're right. And I'm going to talk to him about it. Now."

They pulled to a stop in front of Emerson's house, and Bree drew in a deep breath. This was it. The moment when she would get everything out in the open.

There was no need to sit on these theories any longer. The best thing she could do was to tell Emerson what she'd discovered and see how he reacted.

"Are you ready for this?" Dez asked.

"As ready as I'll ever be."

He offered a quick nod before they climbed out. She noticed Dez glancing around as they walked toward the door. Did he still think that the gunman might be out here? Did he not believe that Trixie's brothers were responsible?

A shiver rippled through her. Bree preferred to think that the person responsible for the attempts on her life was behind bars. It was what had helped her sleep better last night.

As they climbed the steps to the front door, Dez stiffened beside her. "Wait here."

What did he see that Bree didn't?

She peered around him and noticed that the door was cracked open.

That, in itself, was a warning sign. Emerson was from LA. People didn't leave their doors open like that in LA. Certainly, not Emerson.

Bree stood against the side of the building and waited as Dez pushed the door open. He drew his gun and remained on guard as he shoved the door lightly. Looking back, he motioned for her to follow.

Good. Bree really didn't want to stand out here by herself.

"Hello, Emerson?" Dez called. "Is anyone here?"

They heard nothing.

"Stay behind me," Dez whispered.

Bree would have no trouble doing that. In fact, what she had the most trouble with was not holding onto Dez like a lifeline.

Something was wrong here, and she didn't know what.

Emerson's car was in the driveway, so he should be here. There was no reason for him not to be.

They moved through the entryway and checked the four bedrooms downstairs. They were clear. They moved up to the second floor and checked the rooms there. They were also clear. Finally, on the third floor of the house, they found the kitchen and living room.

It was obvious that Emerson had been staying here. The place was a mess, but Emerson had never been known for being neat and tidy. He preferred that other people cleaned up after him.

Dez checked his bedroom, but Emerson wasn't there either.

The place appeared to be clear.

Then where was Emerson? Had something happened to him?

"Is he a runner?" Dez turned toward Bree, gun still in hand but lowered.

"Not since I've known him." Bree shrugged.

"Something is weird about this."

"I agree." Bree wandered over toward the table where some papers had been laid out.

What she saw there took her breath away.

There were pictures of Bree. With Dez. From all over Lantern Beach. Just like the ones someone had sent to her email just yesterday.

But there was more than that. There were also

handwritten threats. Just like the ones she'd received.

Had Emerson been the person responsible for sending her these notes, promising to kill her in inexplicable ways? That was what it looked like.

CHAPTER TWENTY-THREE

DEZ FELT the tension growing inside him. From what he could tell, Emerson was the one behind the chaos surrounding Bree's life over the past few months.

But why? What sense did that make?

Dez had already called Cassidy, and she was on her way. If the man was missing, they needed to file a report. And if he was responsible for the threats, Cassidy needed to arrest him.

As Dez paced away from the breakfast bar, he looked over at Bree. She stood near the window, staring outside. Her face had gone pale, and she couldn't seem to draw her eyes away from the ocean.

He crossed the room until he stood beside her. "What are you thinking?"

Bree squeezed the skin between her eyes. "I don't know what to think. It was one thing when I thought Emerson was a greedy, selfish manipulator. But it's a whole other story if he's the one who's been behind these threats. And, if that's the case, was he also responsible for trying to shoot me? It just doesn't make any sense."

"What if he did this as a publicity stunt?"

She blinked, thought about it for a moment, and then nodded. "Sadly, I wouldn't put it past him. He's always thought that bad publicity was better than no publicity."

She lowered herself into the chair behind her, almost as if her legs couldn't hold her up anymore.

"I'm sorry." Dez's gaze softened. "I know this has to be hard on you."

"I keep thinking that it can't get worse, and then it does. I don't even know what to think anymore."

"Hey . . ." He pulled a chair beside her and sat down.

As his arm wrapped around the back of the chair, Bree leaned into him. Dez pulled her toward him, relishing the feel of her body against his. Savoring her honeysuckle scent. Dreaming about doing this not just right now but for a long time.

Why did this feel so natural? Like they'd done it a million times before? This should feel off-limits.

"You're going to get through this," he murmured, stroking her back.

"Thanks for the vote of confidence." She sniffled. "But I feel like I'm losing my mind."

"I'll be around to help you find it."

"That's awfully nice of you. It's a good thing I paid for the best." Her voice cracked.

Dez pulled her closer, hearing the uncertainty in her voice. She was wondering if he was comforting her out of professional obligation. "This isn't just about me doing my job. You know that, don't you?"

She pulled back until their gazes met. "Then what is this about?"

His heart pounded in his ears as their faces remained only inches apart. He pushed a stray hair behind her ear.

He wanted nothing more than to lean in closer, to feel her lips against his—

"Police!"

It was Cassidy. Her voice had come from downstairs. She was here and ready to take their statements.

Dez and Bree moved back from each other. Dez would be lying if he said he wasn't disappointed.

But Cassidy's arrival had come at just the right time. He didn't want to break the rules by crossing boundaries on the job. He silently thanked Cassidy for stopping him.

Except, he didn't feel entirely thankful right now.

He comforted himself by thinking that maybe the police chief had learned something new, something that would get him off this job and ensure that Bree was safe.

If Emerson was behind this, had he run away out of fear of being caught? Something about that didn't seem quite right. But, if not, what happened to him?

That's what they needed to figure out.

BREE'S THOUGHTS continued to churn. As they did, more anger grew inside her. How could Emerson do this? It just didn't make any sense to her.

"We'll put out a BOLO for Emerson." Cassidy wandered back into the room, easing her phone into her pocket. "He has to be around here somewhere. There's no sign of violence, so that's a good thing."

Bree and Dez sat at the dining room table as they

tried to figure out their next step. Wait for Emerson? Search for him? Call her lawyers again?

"I thought all this was over when you arrested Trixie's brothers," Bree said. "I just can't believe it's still going on."

Cassidy tilted her head. "I know. This one is baffling. But we're not going to stop investigating until we have answers."

As she said the words, they heard footsteps on the stairs. Cassidy drew her gun while Dez moved in front of Bree. Bree braced herself for whoever was coming up the steps. Another police officer would have announced himself.

A moment later, Emerson appeared. His beady gaze wandered around the room as surprise flashed in his eyes.

"What in the world are you all doing here?" he demanded. "And how did you get in?"

"You have some explaining to do." Cassidy held up one of the photos. "What is this all about?"

Emerson's face paled, as if he knew he'd been caught. He shook his head. "It's not what you think."

"Then you'd better start talking," Cassidy said.

CHAPTER TWENTY-FOUR

"I STARTED GETTING these in the mail about three months ago," Emerson said.

Bree narrowed her gaze at him, completely done giving him the benefit of the doubt. "Because you were sending them?"

Emerson's eyebrows shot up as if he was offended at the very notion. He sat across from them at the dining room table, which felt a bit like an interrogation room right now. He was on one side—alone, while Bree, Dez, and Chief Chambers sat across from him.

"No!" Emerson said. "Of course, I wasn't sending them. I was just as surprised as you were to get these."

"But you never mentioned that you were getting these also." Bree hoped she wasn't overstepping by inserting herself into this conversation.

"I knew how it would look so I didn't say anything."

"But the fact alone that you got these as well could have helped the police locate who's behind this," Bree said.

"Look, I know." Emerson ran a hand over the top of his head before leaning forward. "I know, okay? I didn't know what to do so I stayed quiet."

"Why did you stay quiet?" Chief Chambers asked.

"As I said before—I knew how this would look."

"And how is that?" Dez crossed his beefy arms.

"It would make me look like I had something to do with it," Emerson's words collided with each other.

"And did you have something to do with it?" Chief Chambers asked.

"No! Why would I have something to do with this? Bree is my client. What sense would it make?"

"Maybe you were trying to drum up some publicity for my tour?" Bree suggested.

Emerson scoffed at the idea. "I may like publicity, but I wouldn't take it that far."

"Listen, you just need to tell us everything." Chief Chambers locked her gaze on Emerson. "Because you're looking like the bad guy right here."

"Okay, okay, okay! No one's giving me a chance to talk. You guys just keep asking questions . . ." Even while he was being interrogated, Emerson had found a way to manipulate the conversation to make everybody else feel bad.

It was so typical of Emerson.

"I started getting these threats around the same time Bree did, like I already told you. I'm not sure why I was getting them as well as Bree. I just figured somebody wanted to drive home the threats by letting me see them too."

"I'm not buying that," Chief Chambers said. "I'm going to ask you again. Do you have any idea who is sending these threats?"

"I have no idea."

"And everything that you got was exactly the same as what Bree was getting?" Cassidy continued.

Something flashed in Emerson's eyes. The chief had him. There was something that he wasn't saying.

"It seemed like it was almost the same." Emerson frowned.

"What does that mean?" Chief Chamber's voice hardened. "Why don't you just give it to us straight?"

Emerson wiped his brow as a layer of sweat formed there. "The truth is that someone's been blackmailing me."

Bree felt her jaw go slack. "What does that even mean? Blackmailing you how?"

He let out a long breath. "They told me if I didn't pay them, they were going to kill Bree. They sent me these pictures and threats to let me know that they were serious."

"How much money have they been asking for?" Dez asked.

"So far, I've paid out fifty thousand. But I just got another threat this morning. They asked for twenty thousand more. That's where I was. I just made the drop."

"You had twenty thousand on hand?" Chief Chambers stared at him, her disbelief obvious.

"I had some cash on hand. I left my Rolex to pay the rest. It's worth…" He tugged at his collar. "Quite a bit."

"Where did you leave it?" Chief Chambers continued.

"At some controversial land," he muttered. "They said something about Gilead's Cove property. The instructions were specific. I couldn't drive. I had to ride a bike."

"Why was your door unlocked?" Dez asked.

"I don't know. I must have left in a hurry. They only gave me thirty minutes to get there."

"Someone must have known how much money you could get and how quickly," Chief Chambers said.

Emerson nodded. "I suppose they did."

"Why would someone be blackmailing you like this?" Chief Chambers asked.

"Because they know that Bree is my cash cow." Emerson glanced at Bree and grimaced. "Sorry to be crass, but that's the way some people see it. They knew if something happened to you that I would also be hurting."

"That's good to know. It's not because you cared about me or anything," Bree muttered.

"Well, it's that too, of course." Emerson halfway rolled his eyes.

Dez nudged him. "You better show some respect to the lady."

At Dez's deep voice, Emerson straightened and nodded.

A brief moment of delight fluttered through Bree at seeing her manager sweat.

"Because Bree is your 'cash cow' isn't a reason for

blackmail," Chief Chambers said. "There has to be something else."

Emerson's gaze darkened. "They want me to admit that I mistreat people. Confess my sins. In public. And if I don't . . ."

"If you don't what?" Dez asked.

Emerson's gaze fluttered up to Bree's. "Bree will die."

"You never considered going to the police with this information?" Chief Chambers looked downright flabbergasted. "That's what I find so hard to believe. This is a serious threat."

"They said if I told anybody, it was a deal breaker. I didn't want to risk it."

"But you would risk Bree's life?" Dez shook his head, making no effort to disguise his disgust. "You should be thankful right now that there's a police chief present because . . ."

Emerson swallowed hard and rubbed his throat. "I was in a bad position."

"I'd say," Bree muttered. "You chose your own personal success over my life. If I ever had any doubt that you were vile, all of that doubt is now gone."

"It's not like that. I was trying to figure out a solution. I just knew there was something else I could do but . . ." He shrugged. "Then the shooting happened."

Chief Chambers, Dez, and Bree all exchanged looks. The story seemed outlandish. But what if he was telling the truth?

Finally, Chief Chambers looked back at him. "I'm going to need a list of people who might hate you."

Emerson locked his gaze with hers. "I hope you have a while because this could take all day."

DEZ LEANED BACK in the chair and ran a hand across his eyes. This whole day had not turned out the way he'd anticipated. And now Emerson was here with his bizarre tale.

Dez thought that there were pieces of the truth in what the man said. But Dez's gut still told him that there was more to the story that Emerson wasn't sharing.

Emerson had just gone through a list of people who didn't like him, a list so long that Dez was losing interest.

"Let's talk about people who might be here on the island who have a vendetta against you," Cassidy said. "Anybody who fits that bill?"

"Well, yes," Emerson said, as if it was a given. "Trixie Dare, for starters."

Now there was a familiar name.

"Why does Trixie hate you?" Cassidy asked.

Emerson reached into his pocket and pulled out a stress ball. He began working it in his hands. "She was desperate for me to sign her. She told me she would do anything if I would represent her. I told her no, and, as you might imagine, she was very upset."

"How did she react?"

"She said that I would regret it."

Dez watched the man, noting how his stress ball was a yellow smiley face. It didn't fit the man, but maybe it reminded him to try to find joy.

Maybe.

"Did you ever see or hear from her again after that?" Cassidy continued.

"Just at various events around town. She never really spoke to me again, but she could give a man a cold stare across the room."

"Anyone else who comes to mind?"

Emerson squirmed, as if he was suddenly uncomfortable. "There is one other person who was on the island. Bobby Dee."

"Bobby Dee?" Bree's voice rose an octave. "My drummer?"

"The man hates me." He squeezed his stress ball again.

"So why did you bring him on for my band?" Bree asked.

"Because he's one of the best in the business. He knows if he's in one of my bands that he'll have a steady paycheck. But he always wants more. So it makes sense that maybe this was his way of getting more money."

"But Bobby Dee is no longer here on the island, correct?" Bree asked.

"I'm not sure. He certainly doesn't report to me. But whoever is behind this is obviously still on the island. Now, is there anything else that you need? I'm getting a migraine, and Bree can tell you exactly what I'm like when I have one of those."

She resisted an eye roll. Bree wasn't doubting that the man was telling the truth about the migraine. But he was so dramatic and manipulative that she didn't know what to believe right now.

"You're going to need to go down to the station." Cassidy leveled her gaze. "We have some more questions for you."

"Am I being arrested?" Emerson's eyes widened.

"Not yet," Cassidy said. "But your cooperation will be greatly appreciated."

One of her officers arrived and led him away. Bree didn't have a chance to talk to him about her contract or paychecks. That would have to wait until later, she supposed. They had enough other stuff to deal with right now.

CHAPTER TWENTY-FIVE

BREE COULDN'T STOP THINKING about the almost kiss that had happened with Dez. Everything in her had been longing to feel his lips against hers, to know if the chemistry would explode between them.

But the chief had shown up before she and Dez could explore that further.

Bree tried to put it out of her mind and focus on what the police chief was now saying.

Emerson had been taken into custody, but he wasn't being charged yet. The police had enough to hold him while they looked into his background.

Now the chief was putting all her efforts into finding answers.

"Officer Dillinger is at the drop site," Chief

Chambers said. "I want to go down there and check it out myself. There's probably no evidence, but I'd like to put my eyes on the scene."

Dez's eyes met Bree's before he said, "I'd like to go too, if you wouldn't mind. The person behind this is targeting Bree, and it's my job to keep her safe."

"I don't mind tagging along," Bree said. It beat staying here without Dez.

Chief Chambers and Dez exchanged a look before the chief nodded. "That's fine if you come, Bree. As long as you stay close."

A few minutes later, they were all in the chief's police SUV, heading down the road.

"This place—the old location of Gilead's Cove—has a lot of bad memories." Chief Chambers frowned as she gripped the steering wheel. "It's like the very ground is haunted."

"I wasn't here when the cult was around, but I've heard plenty about it," Dez said.

"What's Gilead's Cove?" Bree asked. "I've heard it mentioned a couple of times, and it sounds vaguely familiar but . . ."

"They were a cult that moved to the island last year. They set up camp on a property here," the chief explained. "Things turned ugly. Really ugly. But I'm glad that we had a happy ending. The land, however, is still a source of contention. A developer wants to build a hotel there, and locals are fighting it."

"For a peaceful little island, a lot of trouble seems to head this way." Bree frowned as she stared out the window.

"You've got that right," Chief Chambers muttered.

A few minutes later, they pulled up to a piece of land right on the waters of the Pamlico Sound. A temporary fence had been put up around the property. The space was mainly empty, but Bree could see where, at one time, there had been hookups for campers. A scorched building sat in the middle of it all. This seemed like a stark reminder of the vastness of evil when it got into a person's heart.

"Emerson said he left it on a tree stump." Chief Chambers glanced at Bree in the backseat. "Bree, stay close. I think this area is clear, but we have to be careful."

Bree didn't argue. They climbed from the police car and met another officer who waited in the distance.

"There was nothing here when I arrived," Officer Dillinger said. "Whoever blackmailed Emerson for the money must've been waiting for him to drop it off and not wanting to take any chances."

"I need to ask around and see if anyone in the area saw anything," Cassidy said.

"I can do that. There was one thing I found that I thought was strange." He pulled out a plastic bag with a tube of Chapstick inside. "This was only about a foot away from the site. It looks new. Do you think the person who picked up the money could have dropped it?"

Chief Chambers took the bag from him. "I think it's something worth looking into. Maybe we can run it for DNA as well as for prints."

Bree sighed and glanced around, trying to get into the mind of the person who was making these threats. So much still didn't make sense. "Why did the person who demanded money from Emerson insist that he come here of all places?"

"That's a good question," Dez said. "Maybe it's because it's secluded out here."

"That's a possibility," the chief said. "But there are other secluded places here on the island."

Just as she said the word, a new sound filled the air.

Gunfire.

Again.

Dez dove in front of Bree as another bullet whizzed by.

"WHERE ARE THE SHOTS COMING FROM?" Cassidy yelled, drawing her gun and ducking behind a tree.

"Over there." Dez pointed to the woods in the distance, careful to keep himself in front of Bree. But they both needed to move. Now.

More shots rang out.

Dez pulled Bree to her feet, darted across the sandy ground, and stashed her behind a thick tree. More bullets shot through the air. They splintered the wood around them and pierced the ground.

Cassidy and Braden remained shielded behind two other trees, their guns drawn. During a break from the barrage of bullets—probably because the gunman reloaded—Cassidy turned and fired back.

As soon as she did, more bullets littered the area.

Cassidy tucked herself back behind the tree just in time.

Dez pulled out his weapon and peered around the oak. Whoever was shooting at them was unseen. Maybe he was wearing black and remaining in the shadows or behind the trees. It didn't matter. Either way, he couldn't see the man.

Dez looked at Cassidy. They waited a minute before Cassidy gave Braden the signal.

"We've got to go after him," Cassidy said. "Dez, you stay here with Bree."

He wasn't going to let her out of his sight. He nodded and watched as Cassidy and her officer took off after the man.

"What's happening?" Bree's voice came out quickly. Her eyes were dilated. Her breaths shallow with fear.

"My guess? This person realized they had dropped something here at the site and came back to retrieve it. When they did, they saw us here and decided to take a shot."

"This person really does want me dead, doesn't he?" Bree squeezed her eyes shut.

Dez pulled her closer, in a protective manner. At least, that's what he told himself. But maybe she was just a little too close for it to be professional. He would have to figure that out later.

"He's going to mess up sometime, and we're going to catch him," he muttered.

They waited. The minutes ticked by slowly. Too slowly.

Were they okay out there?

Finally, Cassidy and Officer Dillinger returned with frowns on their faces.

"Whoever it was, he got away." Cassidy frowned. "He had a car waiting in the woods. I knew I couldn't get back to my own vehicle in time, so I called it in. Maybe—just maybe—one of my guys will be able to catch him."

Bree seemed to sag with relief against the tree. "What's that mean for me in the meantime?"

Cassidy frowned but her voice was steady as she said, "It means that you continue to wait. I know it's hard. And it's probably not what you want. But, at this point, it's the only thing that will keep you safe."

Bree frowned, and Dez's heart pounded against his chest as he watched her. Coming face-to-face with death wasn't an easy task.

He knew. Because he had been there one too many times before.

CHAPTER TWENTY-SIX

CASSIDY DROPPED Dez and Bree back off at their car, but instead of returning to Bree's place, Dez asked if they could stop by Ty's house instead.

She agreed, and they headed that way. Dez had gotten a message from Colton saying they needed to talk, and he was anxious to hear what was going on. He knew there was nothing else he could do right now for Bree.

What he wanted was to teach Emerson a lesson. He wanted to track down the owner of that Chapstick. But the best thing he could do was to keep Bree safe.

When they walked into Ty's house, Colton and Elise were sitting on the couch, smiling at each other with warm affection. A moment of envy shot through him.

Would Dez ever find that someone? He knew the answer. Not unless he opened himself up to it. He just wasn't sure he was ready to do that yet.

Colton and Elise stood and walked over to greet them.

"Do you mind if we talk in the office?" Colton asked after a couple minutes of chitchat.

"I'll be happy to keep Bree company," Elise said.

"Ty is working downstairs," Colton said. "He'll keep an eye on the place for us."

With a glance at Bree, Dez nodded. She seemed okay with it, and Dez knew she would be in good hands. He followed Colton into his office and braced himself for whatever he had to say.

To his surprise, a man was sitting there.

A man Dez hadn't seen in a very long time.

"Brian Starks?" Dez muttered.

The man rose and extended his hand. "Long time no see."

If Brian was here, that couldn't be good.

Because Brian was their former commander's chief of staff. If he was here, then something had to be up. Something bad.

"SO, I LOVE YOUR SONGS," Elise told Bree as they fixed some coffee. "It's such a thrill to have you here on the island."

"Thanks." Bree tried to smile but found it hard, considering everything that was going on here lately. It seemed like all she'd caused was trouble. "How long have you been here?"

Elise pulled out some sugar and cream and set it on the counter. "A couple of months. I found myself in a life-or-death situation, not unlike you are right now. There was only one person I could think of who could help me, and that was Colton."

Her curiosity spiked. "You two seem really cute together."

"Thanks. For the longest time, I only knew Colton as my husband's best friend. My husband was killed in the line of duty more than a year ago." Her voice cracked, but she continued pouring her coffee. "I had no idea that something could be there with Colton, but circumstances like mine made things clear very fast."

"I'm sorry for everything that happened, but it sounds like it all had a happy ending." Bree added some cream to her cup, relaxing as the radio played softly in the distance. Music had always had that effect on her.

Elise nodded, a gentle smile feathering across her lips. "The path that brought us together wasn't easy, but I'm glad that we are where we are today."

Bree took a sip of her coffee, and they moved to the table to talk. "Do you help with Blackout now?"

"I'm a psychologist," Elise said. "I'm helping out here by offering a listening ear to any of the guys who come here for Ty's programs. I could see where there was a hole in that area previously, and I am happy to fill in the gap."

"It sounds like everything came together just as it was supposed to."

Elise nodded, crossed her arms on the table, and leaned forward. "So how are you doing, Bree? I know this is a lot for you to take in. I'm not asking as a psychologist. Not officially, at least. I'm asking because you look like you could use someone to talk to."

Bree let out a short breath, wondering how much to say. "If I start talking, I might take up the rest of your day. Maybe even the rest of your week."

"Well, I've got some time."

The invitation seemed to be just what Bree needed. She poured out all of the events from the past few months, leading right up to what she had learned today.

"That sounds like a lot to take in." Elise frowned.

"Tell me about it." Bree shook her head. Sometimes it all seemed surreal. Everything had happened so fast that she could hardly breathe, much less think.

"It must be hard not knowing if someone likes you for you or for what you can do for them."

"Exactly. How am I supposed to know the difference? I really struggle with that."

"I think your heart and your gut can guide you. Plus, watch the actions of the other person. Are they there for you when you need them? Or just in the times that are glamorous?"

Bree took a sip of coffee and replayed the events of the past couple of days. Emerson certainly hadn't been there for her. He was clearly only looking out for himself. Her band had checked on her, but most of them had left to go be with their families. She couldn't blame them after an event like this. Her assistant had called to check on her also, and Bree felt like Karen would be here if it wasn't for her mom's surgery.

And then there was Dez . . . something about him made Bree want to think that he was the real deal. But she had to remind herself that she *was* paying him. All of his actions couldn't be trusted considering he was employed by her right now.

The thought caused a frown to form on her face.

Before Bree could say anything, a song came on the radio, and Bree froze at the sound.

"What is it?" Elise studied her face.

"That's my song," Bree said. "The one I wrote."

"And that's not you singing it, is it?"

Bree felt her jaw go slack. "No, as a matter of fact, it's not. It kind of sounds like . . ."

Before she could finish her statement, the DJ finished it for her. "And that's the new single by Trixie Dare."

Trixie Dare? How had Trixie gotten her hands on Bree's song?

CHAPTER TWENTY-SEVEN

DEZ STARED at Brian in disbelief. He was the last person he'd expected to show up here on Lantern Beach. Something about seeing him now felt off, like something wasn't right.

Did Colton have that feeling also?

"What are you doing here?" Dez asked Brian.

"I didn't know who else I could talk to but you." Brian's face looked tense.

He'd changed from his normal military garb into some jeans and a sweatshirt. But he still carried himself like a sailor, with his back straight, his head raised, and his gaze firm. The man was in his mid-thirties, and his name had been added to their suspect list when Blackout had been searching for a spy within their old military command.

Brian nodded toward the chairs across from him as he silently asked them to sit. Dez lowered himself in one, and Colton sat in the other. He couldn't wait to hear what this man had to say.

He would take everything with a grain of salt, however. "What do you need to talk about?"

"There are whispers that something is going to happen." The words sounded raw and rushed as they left Brian's lips. He rubbed his palms on his jeans, as if they were sweaty.

"Something within what?" Dez asked. "What exactly are you referring to?"

"Within the Savages. I think they're planning something. Planning something big."

Dez shook his head, trying to put the pieces together while remaining cautious. "Jason Perkins is behind bars. They don't have their inside man to plant information or to share it."

"I know. I know what you're saying. But I can't help but think that there's more to it than we know now."

"Why don't you start from the beginning?" Colton said.

"No one will listen to me." Brian swallowed hard, his stiff features showing his stress. "I tried to talk to both the commander and the secretary. They both brushed me off."

"What did you try to tell them, Brian?" Dez asked.

"I overheard them in a meeting." He rubbed his hands against his jeans again. "There have been lots of meetings. The CIA has come in. Something is going on with the Savages, but every time it gets brought up, no one does anything."

"Who is no one?" Colton asked.

"It's . . . no one. It's like everyone is brushing it under the rug."

Colton shifted. "What are you implying?"

"I think there's some kind of coverup going on. I don't know who's involved or who's pulling the strings . . . but I have a hard time believing all of this is over."

"Why come here?"

"From what I heard, the Savages are planning something big. It's going to happen if someone doesn't stop them."

Dez remembered Daniel's final words. *This is only the tip of the iceberg. Be careful who you trust.*

It was like he feared. What if Jason wasn't the only mole planted within the government?

Even worse, what if Brian had come here, not to

help them, but as a plant? What if he was setting up Colton and Dez by handing over this information? When it came to cloak-and-dagger operations, no one could be trusted.

After everything that had happened, Dez couldn't afford to put his faith in the wrong person.

And now the question was what were Dez, Colton, and the rest of the Blackout team going to do with the information Brian had shared?

BREE WAS quiet as she and Dez rode beside each other when they left Ty's place. After she had heard the song, she'd gotten on the phone with her attorney. Normally, she would let Emerson handle something like this, but he obviously couldn't be trusted.

All of this felt bigger than what she was capable of handling. All she wanted was to be a singer. But suddenly all these other problems had popped up, and Bree needed to figure out what to do.

Her attorney was going to work on this now, but she had to question how she was going to even pay him, considering that Emerson hadn't been paying her for the past several months. She'd been so stupid not to look into that herself and to stay on top of it. She was too trusting. That was all there was to it.

"Are you okay?" Dez asked.

She had already told him what had happened, and his jaw had flexed in that familiar manner it did when he didn't like what was being said.

But it was more than that. She wasn't sure what that meeting had been about, the one he'd been called to Ty's house for. But it had left Dez looking unsettled. His gaze looked tumultuous, as if deep into processing something. The twinkle was gone from his eyes, and a smile was nowhere to be seen. She figured it wasn't her business.

"I just don't know what to think anymore," she finally said. "Maybe I should just get out of this business while I can before it ruins me. Maybe my mom and dad were right."

"Or maybe you can be the voice of change. You can be the one who proves that things don't have to change you, but that you can change the world with the platform that you've been given."

She looked at him, surprise filling her eyes. "You really think that?"

"I see your strength in your eyes, Bree. I know all of this has been a lot on you. I know it's been tough, and you're probably questioning yourself. Sure, you probably have a lot of lessons to learn. But we can all say that. I do think that what you've been given is an amazing opportunity."

"Thank you," she finally croaked out.

Emotion clogged her throat. It had been a long time since she had felt like someone would be that honest with her. Dez's sincere words did something to her heart.

She was in trouble. The woman who'd vowed to never fall for a player was obviously falling for a player. And, to make matters worse, it was a player she'd hired to be on her staff.

She cleared her throat as her thoughts shifted. "Listen, would you mind swinging by Bobby Dee's place?"

"Your drummer? Is he still in town?"

"I'm not sure, but I'd like to check. Just in case."

"Sure, we can swing by, if that's what you want."

"I do. I need to talk to someone who's in this business. I'm not sure if Bobby Dee is the right one or not, but he's all I've got right now."

A few minutes later, they pulled up to the cottage where Bobby Dee had been staying. With Dez by her side, she climbed the stairs and knocked at his door. A moment later, Bobby Dee answered. The man was in his late twenties, with a shock of dark hair, striking blue eyes, and a boyish face.

Surprise lined his features when he saw her. "Bree? Didn't expect to see you."

The man looked like he had just woken up. His hair was messy, his clothes sloppy, and his eyes still droopy with sleep.

"Come on in," he said.

They stepped inside his place and saw that it was a wreck. Beer cans everywhere as well as every other type of convenience food wrapper. Was he drowning his sorrows? His guilt?

Bree didn't know.

"A lot of things have been happening since I talked to you last," Bree said.

He nodded toward the couch and moved some of the trash off a couple cushions. "Have a seat. What's going on?"

Bree didn't hesitate before diving in. "Emerson hasn't paid me in six months. How about you?"

A range of emotion flashed in his eyes. Was it surprise? Bree wasn't sure.

"No, man. He's been paying me."

"Are you sure?" Dez asked, his laser-focused gaze on Bobby Dee.

"Yeah, man. I'm sure. That stinks that he hasn't

been paying you. Are you sure that he's not taking out recoupable items?"

"Recoupable items?"

"You know, under contract, the label is allowed to take out of your royalties the expenses they've used for publicity and other things used to build your career."

"I don't know anything for sure," Bree said. "I know that I've been bringing in a lot of profit. And for me to be making hardly anything during this time seems very suspicious. My tours are sold out. Merchandise alone should be bringing in six figures."

Bobby Dee's gaze met hers. His Adam's apple bobbed up and down before he said, "Maybe you should look into Starr Enterprises."

"Starr Enterprises?" Dez asked. "What is that?"

"It's Emerson's other business. He doesn't like to talk about it a lot. But I saw something online and started doing some research on it."

"I had no idea he was involved in other business-es," Bree said. "What is Starr Enterprises exactly?"

"It's a line of hotels that are going to be built across the world." Bobby Dee shrugged, but his shoulders looked tight. "Emerson is behind them."

"That sounds like something that will need a lot of capital," Dez said.

"You can say that again," Bobby Dee muttered.

Dez's phone buzzed, and he stepped away for a second. As he did, Bree made casual chitchat with Bobby Dee. She'd thought her drummer's reaction would be stronger to what she told him. Usually someone like Emerson would take all his clients for a ride, not just one of them. And based on what Carson had told her . . .

When Dez returned to the room, he had a strange look in his eyes. His gaze remained on Bobby Dee.

"That was the chief of police," he started. "She was calling to let us know that Trixie Dare has been cleared and released from jail."

"How is that possible?" Bree felt the air drain from her lungs.

"Turns out she has an alibi for the time during some of the crimes."

"An alibi?" Bree asked.

Dez's gaze went to Bobby Dee. "With your drummer."

BREE WATCHED the shock roll across Bobby Dee's face. At once, the man shook his hands in the air, as if trying to stop an army of renegades from coming at him. Dez's words had definitely shaken him up.

"It's not like it sounds, man." He leaned back, as if trying to distance himself.

"Then how is it?" Dez loomed closer, his intimidating presence making Bobby Dee shrivel even more.

"Yes, Trixie and I did have a thing going on." Sweat spread across his forehead.

"But you have a girlfriend back home." Bree shook her head, her faith in men dying a little bit more.

"I know. I know, all right? I didn't say it was

something I'm proud of. But Zoe knew when she hooked up with me that I had a wandering eye. It was an . . . an *agreement* we had."

"You're saying that Zoe is okay with you being with other women while you two are dating?" Bree felt sick to her stomach as the words left her lips. She'd known Bobby Dee liked to party, but she'd had no idea he'd gone this far.

Bobby Dee shrugged. "Yeah, that's basically what I'm saying."

"And Trixie was your choice?" Bree didn't like where all of this was going.

"That's right. Trixie is cute, and she's fine. She's using me and I'm using her, and we're both okay with it."

Another thought slammed into Bree's mind. "Bobby Dee, did you ever let Trixie hear that song we played around with?" Bree asked.

His eyes widened. "Which one are you talking about?"

"The one I wrote about love being like an ocean on a cloudless, beautiful day."

Dez knew where this was going, and he didn't like it.

Bobby Dee's face turned another shade paler. "I don't know. I don't remember. Why?"

"Because she stole that song from me and recorded it. I was trying to figure out where in the world she could've gotten her hands on that. The only people who had ever heard me play it were you and Lloyd." She leaned closer. "Bobby Dee?"

He looked away, an obvious sign of guilt.

"I may have let her listen to it once a few months ago. But she would have never stolen it."

"I'm telling you, she did steal it. It was just on the radio."

Bobby Dee's eyes widened even more. "Oh, Bree . . . I am so sorry. I had no idea."

"No, I guess you didn't. You had more important priorities, didn't you?"

"I've messed up."

"There's more to this," Dez said. "What aren't you telling us?"

"Nothing. What else could I have to tell you? Everything you've heard is already bad enough, isn't it?"

"I don't believe you when you say that Emerson is treating you right. Tell us the truth."

Bobby Dee looked away again and let out a long breath. "He's been blackmailing me. He threatened to tell Zoe about my extracurricular activities in return for my silence."

"Your silence over what?" Bree's voice climbed in pitch.

"I knew he wasn't doing right by the band. By you. I overheard a conversation he was having once, and it became clear. He's taking our money and using it for these other investments. It's almost like a Ponzi scheme of sorts."

"And you just sat on that information?" Dez shook his head.

Bobby Dee didn't say anything for a moment. Instead, his gaze jerked back and forth with thought. Finally, he said, "My girlfriend really doesn't know about my indiscretions, okay? That was a lie. He was going to tell her. I can't lose her. But I get so lonely here on the road by myself."

"That's a pitiful excuse." Bree shook her head, not disguising how she felt.

"I know." Bobby Dee hung his head down low. "How can I make this right?"

BREE WAS quiet as she climbed back into Dez's car. He made no move to leave. Instead, he just sat there with her for a moment.

"Why do men do the things they do?" she finally asked.

So many thoughts swirled in her head. She almost didn't know which one to pick. Her song being stolen? Her drummer betraying her? Her manager being wrapped up in a possible Ponzi scheme?

But, instead, her thoughts had gone back to Bobby Dee's behavior. It matched that of so many people from her past. Were there actually any good men out there? She was beginning to think there weren't.

"I don't know what to tell you." Dez shifted to face her, his voice soft with concern.

"Are there actually guys who care about the women they're with? Or do they all just want what's best for themselves?"

Dez's hand covered her shoulder. "There are still good guys out there, Bree. I promise."

"Why do you sound so sure?" She tried to ignore his touch, to ignore the electricity she felt whenever he was around. Hadn't she learned any lessons yet? Or would she continue to be too trusting—with both her career and with men?

"Because I know a few of them. There are men out there who care more about commitment and honor than they do about chasing the next thing. Maybe they're harder to find in your line of work, but they do exist."

Bree ran a hand over her face, feeling completely overwhelmed at the situation. But she was so glad that Dez had been there. Despite the walls she wanted to put around her heart, Dez made her feel things she hadn't experienced in a long time. He helped her forget her troubles. Her insecurities. Her doubts.

And there was a lot to be said about that.

"You're the kind of guy people like me write songs about, you know?" she murmured.

She wasn't sure, but it almost looked like Dez blushed.

"Is that right?" A sparkle filled his gaze and a soft smile pulled at his lips.

She nodded, wanting more than anything to kiss him right now. But she didn't. She couldn't. "Yes, it is."

"Well, I'm glad I can inspire someone to do something. But I'm far from perfect, Bree."

"How so?" She waited, eager to see if he'd answer.

"I was supposed to cover my SEAL team leader when we were . . . training. I failed. He died."

She reached out and squeezed his arm. "I'm sorry, Dez."

"And this kind of life I live . . . it isn't for everyone."

"You mean, it wasn't for someone in your past?"

He shrugged. "You could say that. The one woman I gave my heart to broke it. Said I was fun to date but I couldn't support the lifestyle she wanted."

"It sounds like she wasn't the one for you then."

A soft smile played on his face. "I guess she wasn't."

Dez was paid, Bree reminded herself again. At least, she was *supposed* to pay him. Again, she was going to have to figure out her finances really soon. How many more bills was she behind on?

A car pulled up beside them. Bree held her breath when she saw Jill step out. Would she receive another verbal lashing? She braced herself.

As Jill climbed from the car, her gaze went to Bree. She stormed toward them and paused by Bree's door. After a moment of hesitation, Bree put her window down.

"How's Lloyd?" Bree asked.

"He's being released. I just came back here to get some clothes for him."

"That's good news."

Jill stared at Bree another moment before sighing. "Look, I'm sorry for what I said to you earlier. I was a little emotional, and I was worried about Lloyd. I shouldn't have taken it out on you."

Surprise filled Bree, and she nodded. "It's understandable."

Jill took a step back and pointed to the house. "I should go."

"Give Lloyd my best."

"I know he'll want to see you when he gets settled."

"As soon as he says the word, I'll be there."

Jill waved before walking toward the cottage. Bree released her breath. That had gone better than she'd thought. And Lloyd was doing better. At least it was a small amount of good news. She'd take what she could get.

Dez cleared his throat, shifting back to the present. "Where to now?"

"I say we go back to my place. At least for now. I need to clear my head."

CHAPTER TWENTY-NINE

DEZ STOOD IN THE KITCHEN, ready to make *picadillo*, a Cuban rice dish, for lunch. Benjamin had dropped off the ingredients earlier. As Dez filled a pot with water at the sink, he hoped having a brief mental break would be a nice distraction.

As he did, his gaze remained on Bree. She sat at the table across the room, numerous papers in front of her, as well as her laptop computer and her cell phone. She'd been on the phone for most of the day since they'd been back, talking to her attorney and financial manager. She had a lot of things that she needed to work out.

She'd been a surprising tower of strength in the middle of a very stressful situation today. The woman continued to impress him.

Maybe she wasn't anything like Leah. Leah fled when the going got tough. She looked out for herself. Her first thought during a tragedy wouldn't be to look out for the needs of other people.

Maybe he had Bree all wrong from the start.

"Your pot's overflowing, man."

He swerved his head toward Griff's voice. His friend looked down into the sink. Dez followed his gaze and saw that the pan was dripping all over the counter. He quickly turned the water off and grabbed a towel to clean it up.

"Distracted?" Griff asked with a smile.

"More like lost in thought."

Griff let out a little grunt that clearly stated he didn't believe him. Dez couldn't argue that his eyes had been on Bree. He couldn't deny that. Nor could he deny his attraction to the woman.

He tried to remind himself to keep it professional. But every time she touched him, all of those thoughts went out the window.

Griff lowered his voice. "Did you talk to Colton?"

Dez nodded. "Yeah, he called me into his office today."

"Brian Starks, huh?"

Dez put the pot on the stove. "Yeah, I was just as surprised as you are."

"It sounds like trouble is still brewing."

"Did you ever hear back from your friend Anderson?"

"Not yet. But he's still keeping his ears open. He'll let us know if he discovers anything."

Dez's phone rang. It was Colton.

"You'll never believe this," he said. "I just received word that Brian was in an accident on his way home."

Dez's spine stiffened. "What?"

"He left here about the same time you did, wanting to get back before anyone noticed where he had gone. But Cassidy called and let me know that there was a car accident right before the ferry. Brian hit a phone pole. He's being life flighted to a hospital in Raleigh right now. He's unconscious."

"It can't be a coincidence." Dez's gaze met Griff's, letting him know something was wrong. It looked like their Blackout team still had their work cut out for them.

"My thoughts exactly," Colton said. "I have a feeling trouble is still brewing around the Savages. We're going to need to keep our eyes wide open."

BREE HAD BEEN on the phone for so long that her head was beginning to spin. There was so much that still would need to take place before she made any progress on the mess around her. Her attorney had things to look into, as did her financial advisor and her record label.

She stood and stretched. Had two hours really passed since she started making all these phone calls?

Dez's eyes met hers from across the room and he lifted a bowl. "I made some picadillo for you."

"Picadillo?"

He brought a serving over to her. "It's a traditional Cuban rice dish. It has olives, raisins and some spices. I thought you might like it."

Bree held it to her nose. "It smells delicious."

He shrugged and sat across from her. "You said you were a closet foodie, so I thought you might want to try it."

She paused before taking a bite. Dez had a strange look in his eyes that she was trying to read. She'd seen him get that phone call. Saw the looks he and Griff had exchanged. "You look like you got more bad news."

"I did. That man I met with earlier at Ty's . . . he was in an accident as he was leaving the island."

Bree sucked in a breath. "I'm so sorry to hear that. Was he your friend?"

"More like an acquaintance. But he put a lot on the line to come here, and I didn't want something like this to happen."

"I hope he'll be okay."

"Me too." He released a long breath and nodded toward her bowl. "Now, onto some happy news for a minute. What do you think of the rice?"

She took a bite and let the flavors wash over her. Salty olives. Sweet raisins. Spicy cayenne. "Actually, it's delicious. You need to tell your friend down at The Crazy Chefette to add this to her menu. People would love it."

He grinned. "Thank you. My mom would be proud."

"So you're a Navy SEAL, a bodyguard, a singer, and a cook. Is there anything else you can do?"

He stared at her, that grin still playing across his lips. "I may have a few other tricks up my sleeve."

"Is that right?" She cocked an eyebrow.

"Maybe one day when I'm not working for you, I'll show you."

Warmth spread through her chest at the thought of staying in touch with him when this was all over. "I would like that."

They stared at each other another moment, something passing between them.

She had no doubt that there was definitely something there. And Dez felt it too. She felt sure of it.

Bree knew that the two were an unlikely match. But wasn't that how life worked sometimes? Was she really willing to give romance and a relationship another chance?

Or maybe the bigger question should be, was Dez?

She opened her mouth, unsure what was about to come out. Before anything could be said, her phone buzzed.

They both seemed to snap out of the moment. She looked at the screen and saw she had a text.

It was a video. She held her breath before pressing Play. A moment later, Trixie Dare appeared on the screen. There was a gag over her mouth and tears streaming from her eyes as she stared at the screen.

The words beneath the video read: **Come to the lighthouse in 30 minutes. Come alone. Don't be late or she will die.**

CHAPTER THIRTY

"THERE'S no way you can go there alone," Dez said. The image and words from that message burned into his mind. Someone was playing a deadly game right now, and he didn't like it.

"But if I don't, Trixie will die," Bree said. "I may not like the woman, but I don't want to live the rest of my life with her death on my shoulders. I have to go. Alone."

He shook his head, unwilling to let this drop. "I'm going with you."

"I don't know . . ." Bree frowned as she looked at the phone, no doubt remembering the words and image there.

"This could have a very bad ending, Bree." He

had to get through to her before she did anything foolish.

Bree's wide-eyed gaze met his. The swirling depths of her eyes made it clear she understood how serious this could be. What he didn't know was if it was peace or resignation lurking there.

"What do you think this person wants with me when I get there?" she asked.

"Considering that he tried to kill you twice, nothing good."

Bree visibly shuddered and squeezed her eyes shut. "I have to do this."

Part of Dez wanted to lock Bree in a room and not let her go. He wanted to take matters into his own hands. This situation was bad. But he also knew that he couldn't stop her. This was her choice, whether he liked it or not. He could try to convince her to at least take some safety precautions.

"If you show up unarmed and this guy has a gun . . . you're a goner." He didn't mince his words. She needed to know what she was getting into.

Bree raked a hand through her hair and released a long breath. "If this is all about Emerson, I just don't know why this person would need to hurt me anymore. Emerson is being held at the police station. Soon, charges will probably be filed and the whole world will probably know what he's been up to."

"Maybe there's more to the story than we know."

She stood, a determined look in her gaze. "I don't have much time to sit here and talk about it. If I'm going to go, I need to go."

Dez's thoughts raced through all the possibilities. If she was going to do this, she needed to be ahead of the game. "What if we call Cassidy? Her guys could hide out in the woods. This guy doesn't even have to know that they're there."

"He seems to know everything. I don't know how we would keep that from him."

"They could be subtle. But I need to make the call. Now."

Bree stared at him a minute before finally nodding. "Okay, do it. But do it fast because I don't like where any of this is going."

BREE FELT the anxiety rising in her. She didn't want to do this any more than Dez didn't want her to do this. But she had no choice. Certainly, the person behind these threats had known that. He'd known that as soon as Bree realized somebody else was in danger, she'd do whatever she could to help out.

As Dez drove her to the lighthouse, she nibbled on her fingernails—a habit her mom had always hated. But her nerves were getting the best of her. She didn't know what else to do but comply.

When this person discovered Dez was with her, Bree wasn't sure how he would react. But she knew if she went alone, she'd be a sitting duck. Her thoughts battled each other, and her fear only made the war more fierce.

Bree had some decisions to make. One wrong move, and someone could die—including her. The thought didn't make her feel better.

As soon as they pulled up to the lighthouse, Bree looked down at her phone and saw she had another text. She read the words on her screen.

I see you didn't come alone. Go to the top of the lighthouse where there will be more instructions. If your boyfriend goes with you, Trixie will die.

Sweat sprinkled across Bree's skin. This guy had made his position very clear. He wanted her to come alone. If she didn't, there would be consequences.

What should she do?

Dread pooled in her stomach as she and Dez climbed from the car and walked across the sand to the door to the lighthouse. Bree could only assume it would be unlocked.

She climbed the three steps to the door and tugged. It creaked open.

Nausea turned in Bree's stomach. This was it. The moment she had to make a decision.

She paused in the doorway and looked up at Dez.

He tilted his head, seeming to read her mind, before asking, "What?"

How could someone she had only known for a few days come to mean this much to her? It didn't make much sense, but Bree knew whatever it was between the two of them was true, that it was real.

"You know how you have a policy against dating people you work for?" Her heart lodged in her throat as she asked the question.

A knot formed between Dez's eyes as he nodded. "I'm aware."

"Well . . . you're fired."

Before he could respond, Bree reached up and pressed her lips to his.

He stiffened for just a moment before pulling her

closer and deepening the kiss. Bliss spread through her. Yes, there was definitely chemistry there. Pulse-pounding, zings-through-the-blood chemistry.

As they stepped away from each other, their gazes locked. Bree felt nearly breathless as she stared up at him.

"That was a surprise," Dez murmured. "A nice surprise."

Bree nodded. But as soon as she remembered the situation at hand, all her warm fuzzies cooled. She wished this was it, the beginning of a beautiful love story. But there was so much more at hand right now. The beginning might also be the end.

"I really like you, Dez." Her voice sounded raw with emotion. "Thank you for everything."

Before he could say anything, Bree slipped inside the lighthouse and slammed the door. She turned the lock, ensuring Dez couldn't get inside. Regret squeezed her so hard that moisture welled in her eyes.

He pounded on the door. "Bree? What are you doing?"

"I'm sorry," she said. "But it has to be this way."

"No, it doesn't," he called back, his voice urgent, almost desperate. "Let me go with you. Don't let it end this way."

She didn't answer him. She knew she might break down if she did, that she might give in. She couldn't afford for that to happen.

With trembling hands, Bree climbed the dark staircase. The metal steps spiraled and spiraled and spiraled until finally light from above peeked through. The hatch at the very top had been left open for her. It appeared somebody was waiting for her to come.

Her nausea grew stronger until Bree thought she might actually throw up. Would this be a poetic way for her to die? Did death at a young age ensure that she became legendary?

Bree really didn't care about those things. She wasn't sure why the thoughts raced through her mind now. It was nerves, she supposed. All she knew was that she really wanted to survive.

She needed to get her career ironed out. She wanted to get to know Dez better. She wanted to see justice for Emerson.

But she'd been pulled into this deadly game, and now Bree needed to see how it worked out.

As she climbed from the glass enclosure onto the metal deck that surrounded it, a tremble raked through her body. The lighthouse was out on a jetty of sand that extended into the water. On three sides, she saw the ocean raging around her. On any other day, it would be breathtaking.

Bree supposed if she died today, there were worse places to go. The flippant thought didn't comfort her.

The wind swept around the top with surprising force. As she glanced down, she saw a pair of handcuffs had been left there.

Her breath caught. Had those been left for her? She didn't want to know.

"Bree!" She heard Dez yell at her from down below.

She tried to shut out his voice. He would only try to talk her out of doing this. That wasn't a possibility. She'd been left with no other choice. But why was she up here? What now?

Her phone buzzed. The person behind this obviously watched her right now and had seen Bree reach the top. She read the message there.

Livestream to your VideoStream page. Tell the world what Emerson has done to you. But first, place one handcuff around your wrist and the other around the railing. I don't want you to go anywhere.

Maybe Bree could have handled the live video. But handcuffing herself up here? How would she be able to get down? Or maybe that was the point.

Maybe Bree *wouldn't* be getting down.

She didn't know what was about to happen. And she didn't like it.

CHAPTER THIRTY-ONE

DEZ FELT like he was beside himself as he stared up at the top of the lighthouse and called Bree's name. What had she been thinking?

He didn't really have to ask that question. He knew *exactly* what she was thinking. She didn't want to see him—or anyone else—get hurt.

Bree thought this was her problem and that she needed to handle it. Couldn't she understand that Dez wanted to carry these burdens with her?

He pressed his lips together, still trying to catch sight of her. As he did, memories flooded him.

That kiss . . . not only had it been fantastic, but it had also been goodbye, hadn't it? She didn't know how this was all going to turn out. To be truthful, neither did Dez.

He stared at Bree as she stood at the top of the lighthouse. What was she doing? What kind of instructions was this man giving her now?

Oh, Bree . . .

His phone buzzed. It was Cassidy. She and her guys were in place in the woods and out of sight.

Dez wasn't sure if they would be much help at this point. Not with Bree being at the top of the lighthouse and everyone else locked out.

Just what was this guy planning?

He watched from his vantage point below. What was Bree doing? It almost looked like she was putting some kind of bracelet around her wrist.

No, that wasn't a bracelet. It was . . . handcuffs. She was handcuffing herself to the railing. What sense did that make?

Dez didn't know, but the bad feeling in his gut only continued to grow.

"Bree!" he called again.

She looked down but only for a moment. Then she raised her phone and turned to face it. Was she shooting a video?

Dez pulled up her VideoStream channel on his phone. A moment later, a live video started.

"This is Bree Jordan," she said, her voice trembling. The wind hit the microphone, making it hard to understand everything being said. Dez saw the fear in her eyes, the trepidation.

"For the past six months, my manager, Emerson Platt, has been withholding my pay from me. In the meantime, he has been investing in a fictitious company that claims to be building hotels across the world. He's sadly been underpaying his band members. He chose his own well-being over others', which is what has led me to this moment."

She turned the camera so everybody could see just how far from the ground that she was.

Dez felt his head spin as he watched. This was dangerous, with or without the threats against her. A bad feeling pooled in his gut.

Who was behind this? Trixie appeared to have been abducted. Emerson was behind bars. Who else could it be? Bobby Dee? He was the only other person who came to mind.

Dez's phone buzzed again. He quickly read the text from Cassidy.

We ran fingerprints from that tube of Chapstick. And we have a match.

BREE FINISHED HER VIDEO. She'd said every-thing she'd been instructed to say. But, before she stopped recording, she stared at the screen for a moment.

"I just want to say, I am so thankful for the people who have stood by me in the good times and in the bad." Though she tried to stop it, her voice trembled. "I could probably count all of you on one hand, and I want to let you know how much your friendship has meant to me."

She swallowed hard, gathering her thoughts before continuing.

"This is a hard business, a business where you never know who your true friends are. It's become clear that most people in my life look out only for themselves. True success can be measured by the people who truly care about you—and that's some-thing I would have liked to work on. To my fans, your support has meant the world. Thank you for listening. I'm not sure how all of this is going to turn out. But—"

Before Bree could finish her statement, gunfire rang out.

Her phone dropped from her hands, bounced across the metal, and skittered inside the lighthouse. Bree reached for it, but the device was too far away.

Another bullet flew through the air.

Sweat covered her skin. There was nowhere Bree could go from here. Nowhere. She was out in the wide open.

Had the person behind this planned it this way?

But why? Bree had gone on camera and had shared with the world everything about Emerson. His career should be ruined. So why was this person still involving Bree? There had to be more to this. This person also had a vendetta against Bree.

But who could it be? Nothing made sense.

Another bullet hit the metal near her. It pinged, almost sounding like it ricocheted. Glass shattered on the globe of the historic lighthouse.

Bree screamed and tried to duck. But there was nowhere for her to go.

Dez yelled again from down below. He was watching all of this—no doubt in horror.

"I'm so sorry," she whispered. Bree didn't want anyone to see her go like this.

As another bullet rang out, Bree continued to whisper her prayers.

CHAPTER THIRTY-TWO

DEZ GLANCED AROUND. Where was the gunman? Did Cassidy have eyes on him?

He couldn't be sure. But he was certain Bree was an open target right now. The only thing she had going for her was the sheer height of the structure. If he remembered correctly, the lighthouse was almost two hundred feet tall.

Standing near the lighthouse was doing him no good. Dez could very easily become the next target. If he were shot, he'd be useless.

He needed to find the shooter and stop him.

Gripping his gun, Dez darted toward his car. It would offer a shield until he could reach the woods.

As he sprinted behind the vehicle and ducked, his phone rang. It was Cassidy.

"The shooter appears to be in the north end of the woods," she said.

"Are any of your guys over that way?" Dez asked.

"Banks is heading that way now."

"I'm going there too."

"Let's just keep praying that none of those bullets hit Bree."

As Dez got closer, he heard Banks yell. Another gunshot filled the air. Someone let out a shout and then...

A man stumbled from the woods and sprawled on the ground, grasping his chest.

Was that . . . Lloyd? The man's fingerprint had been found on that Chapstick. That's what Cassidy had texted him. Dez shouldn't be surprised to see him.

Banks lowered his gun, a shell-shocked look on his face. Banks had shot Lloyd, hadn't he?

The rookie officer stood there, staring at the man, and most likely feeling stunned over what he'd done.

Dez rushed toward Lloyd and knelt beside the man. Wasting no time, he asked, "Is there something else that's going to happen here today?"

Lloyd stared at him, his eyes wide as they latched

onto Dez's. He opened his mouth as if he wanted to say something. But no words emerged.

"Lloyd, stay with me," Dez ordered.

The man started to mumble something. But, before he could finish the sentence, his eyes closed. He'd lost consciousness.

Dez let out a long breath.

He looked up at the lighthouse again. He had to figure out how to get Bree down.

Because there had to be a reason Lloyd had wanted her up there.

As Cassidy rushed toward Lloyd, Dez took off toward the door.

BREE'S HEART pounded in her ears. There was gunfire. Lots of gunfire.

Dez . . . was he okay? She couldn't live with herself if something happened to him. The whole point of her coming here by herself was that she would be the one to get hurt and not anybody she cared about.

She spotted her phone and stretched her arm out to grab it. Her muscles burned.

It was no use. She couldn't reach the device. Her arm wasn't long enough.

Slouching on the floor, she turned back toward the wooded area in the distance. Someone lay on the ground there.

Was that . . . Lloyd?

Had Lloyd been behind this the whole time? But . . .why? Why would he do something like this? Lloyd had been her friend.

And where was Dez? Was he okay?

Bree scanned everything below her, trying to catch sight of him.

She spotted Officer Banks bending near Lloyd. Chief Chambers ran toward them. But not Dez.

At that moment, a new sound filled the air. Were those footsteps coming up the lighthouse stairs?

Dez. It had to be Dez.

How had he gotten inside? Bree had locked the door.

Someone must have had a key. It was the only thing that made sense.

Could this really be over?

Bree wanted to believe it. She really did.

But a niggling feeling inside her reminded her to remain on guard.

CHAPTER THIRTY-THREE

AS DEZ STARTED BACK toward the lighthouse, he paused. Something wasn't right.

Something like the fact that he hadn't seen a gun in Lloyd's hand. So how was the man shooting? Had he dropped the gun in the woods after he'd been shot?

He looked back to Cassidy and Banks as they leaned over the man's body. Cassidy had her phone to her ear, no doubt calling for backup. She was probably thinking the same thing Dez was.

They were missing something.

Dez glanced around, looking for a sign of trouble. He saw nobody. But that didn't mean the trouble wasn't out there.

"I don't think Lloyd was the shooter," Cassidy called.

Dez's stomach hardened. "Then where is he?"

Was whoever had done this on the run now? Did he think he'd gotten away with this?

Dez was torn between going after the person or trying to get Bree down. But she'd locked herself in that lighthouse. She should be safe . . . right?

He couldn't be entirely sure.

He looked up to inspect Bree again.

Just as he did, a new figure appeared on the walkway around the lighthouse.

He squinted, trying to see who it was.

But before he could, another round of gunfire emerged, and he ran for cover.

BREE'S EYES widened when she saw someone emerge from the hatch on top of the lighthouse. She sucked in a breath, certain she was seeing things.

But she wasn't.

"Jill . . ." she muttered.

Jill climbed up onto the walkway but remained out of reach. The smile on Jill's face caused Bree's insides to squeeze with fear.

She held something in each of her hands—a handgun in one and some kind of remote in the other.

More gunfire sounded from below, and Bree instinctively ducked. Then her eyes widened. If somebody was shooting down there, then who else was Jill working with?

"You didn't think it was going to be that easy, did you?" Jill grinned again.

"How did you get inside? I locked the door." Bree backed against the railing and gripped it.

"I've been inside the whole time. Just waiting patiently. They say good things come to those who wait."

But . . . "If you're in here, who else is down there?"

Satisfaction glimmered in her eyes. "I'll never tell. I'll have to let you and your little boyfriend figure that out."

Bree tugged at her handcuff, wishing desperately she could slip her hand through it. "Why are you doing this, Jill? Didn't you already get what you wanted? I thought Emerson was the target here."

"Emerson was my main target. Thank you for all of your help in exposing his evil deeds. I didn't know the best way to exact my revenge on him, but you helped greatly. I checked and your video already has over 100,000 views. I have a feeling Emerson will be going away for a long time."

"Okay. You got your revenge. Why not just let me go? Why continue to try to hurt people?" Bree glanced below. "Chief Chambers, Officer Banks, Dez . . . they didn't do anything. Can't you call this other shooter off?"

Jill's grin widened. "Sorry. But that's not how this is going to work. I'm so tired of being mistreated. So, so tired."

"Who else has mistreated you?" Bree tried to put the pieces together, tried to buy herself some time. She tugged on her handcuff, wishing desperately it would come loose. But that wasn't going to happen. Until she had a key, she was at Jill's mercy.

Based on the woman's body language, Jill had a plan all worked out.

"You don't even know, do you?" Jill asked.

"Know what?" Bree had no idea what she was talking about.

"You don't see the way Lloyd looks at you."

Bree shrugged. "Lloyd looks at me like a fellow musician."

Jill scoffed. "Then you really are naïve. I thought that show business would've woken you up by now."

"I'm telling you, Jill, Lloyd and I are just friends. There's nothing there but professional respect."

"You may feel that way, but he doesn't. You are all he talks about. I told him not to go on tour with you. One reason was the money. There was so little of it. But the other was because his eyes lit up whenever you were around. I knew what was coming. I could see the writing on the wall. He insisted he do this, despite what I wanted."

Bree tugged at her handcuff again, hating the feeling of being trapped, of feeling helpless. "So why are you punishing me for that? I never did anything inappropriate or gave him any hints that there could be something between us."

Her smile disappeared. "You epitomize everything that I am against. You're pretty, successful, rich, and famous. Frankly, I'm just sick of it. Sick of working so hard for nothing while people like you get what I want, what I deserve."

"So you're going to kill me?"

Jill stepped closer and narrowed her eyes. "I'm thinking about it."

CHAPTER THIRTY-FOUR

WHERE WAS the gunfire coming from? Dez remained on the ground, unwilling to stand yet. Not until he knew where the shooter was. From what he could tell, the gunman wasn't moving around but seemed stationary. Maybe if he went around to the backside of the woods, he could figure out who this person was.

He made eye contact with Cassidy and motioned what he was going to do. She nodded.

A moment later, Dez ducked into the woods. The brush was thick and thorny and occasionally even marshy. Those things were the least of his concerns right now. He had to be quick, efficient, and quiet.

He moved between the trees, careful to conceal

his presence. He didn't want to alert whoever was out here to the fact that he was coming.

Another round of gunfire emerged. *Bang. Bang. Bang.*

It was an automatic weapon, for sure. But something seemed weird about the cadence of the gunshots. It didn't really make any sense. When someone fired again, there wasn't a pattern to the way the person shot.

But something bothered him, and Dez needed to figure out what it was.

As he got closer to the sound, he crouched lower, remaining careful of his footsteps and any sound he might make.

He still didn't see anybody.

But he could smell the gunpowder.

He was close.

Finally, he reached the area where the shots were coming from. And what he saw there made his jaw drop.

"WHY DON'T you just get this over with?" Bree stared at Jill, trying to anticipate her next move. "Why draw it out?"

"I've been living like this for the past six months since you went on tour. Why should it all be over for you so quickly?"

The woman definitely held a grudge, to say the least. Bree needed to keep her talking. "Were you the one who killed Kyle?"

"I was sneaking into Emerson's house to leave him a new threat when Kyle saw me. I had no choice."

"How did you get into my house to leave your threat? How did you get the code?" Bree might as well get some answers as she bought herself time.

"Easy. When you first checked in to this house of yours, all the guys came by for a quick jam session. When you let them in, you punched in the code in front of all of them. Bobby Dee saw you do it. I was talking to Lloyd before the concert—on the phone— when Bobby Dee made a joke about it in the background. I heard him. He even recited the code. Good thing I have a decent memory. When I saw you leave, I went to your house and gave it a try. What do you know? It worked."

If Bree got out of this alive, she made a mental note to be more careful. "And you were the one who opened fire at the concert? You were actually so angry that you decided to shoot into a crowd?"

"I was only aiming for you. Be thankful that I'm a bad shot."

"That took a lot of planning. I'm surprised nobody noticed you were in town and that you were able to get that boat and the guns."

"My dad was an avid fisherman and hunter. He taught me everything I know, including how to shoot and how to operate a boat. It really wasn't that hard. In fact, I put everything I needed in my trunk, took the ferry over, and stayed in a campground until I got the call from you saying that Lloyd had been shot and that I should come. It was all a lot easier than you might think. Plus, nobody was looking for me because nobody suspected I was in town."

"Where's Trixie?" Bree asked, still trying to buy time. She glanced down, trying to guess what was going on below her. It was no use.

"She's in my cabin. She's okay. For now. I'm kind of hoping no one will discover her for a long time, though. She's driving me crazy with that attitude of hers. Maybe I targeted the wrong person, but it's too late now. She stole your song, you know."

"I heard." Bree licked her lips. "You're clever, I'll give you that. You should take that cleverness and put it to good use, not by doing stuff like this."

More gunfire rang out, and Bree ducked again.

Jill let out a laugh aloud, entirely too amused. "You still haven't figured it out? Well, let me give you a little hint. I work by myself."

How was that possible? "Lloyd wasn't in on this?"

"No, he would have never done something like this. Especially not if you were involved. That's why I had to make it look like he was, though. Did you know they have these handy dandy guns that work by remote control? Hunters use them all the time. They set them up in the woods and people who can't leave their homes to hunt can pay to shoot things remotely. Pretty handy, huh?"

"So you're the one who is firing down there?"

She showed Bree the remote. "That's right."

"You are clever. But why hurt more innocent people?"

"Those people never did anything for me. I'm over it all. I'll probably go to jail. I don't think I'm going to get away with all of this, so I might as well enjoy myself on the way out."

"There has to be a different way than this," Bree said. "It's not too late to make things right."

Jill cackled again. "Oh, I would say that it is. I opened fire at a public event. There's no way that I am not going away for life."

That's when Bree realized that Jill wasn't bluffing. There was nothing to hold her back anymore. Bree dreaded to think what that might mean for her.

CHAPTER THIRTY-FIVE

DEZ GRABBED the gun that had been positioned on the tree. He pulled the ammunition out before it could be fired anymore.

A remote control gun? Whoever had come up with this idea was sick. He'd heard of hunters using things like this, but he never thought he'd see it used in a situation like this.

Most likely, whoever was in the lighthouse was using some kind of remote system to operate this. But no more, not without the ammunition.

Dez darted back through the woods, toward Cassidy and Banks. He needed to let them know what was going on, and they needed to figure out a way to get to Bree.

As he emerged from the brush, he filled them in.

"I called Austin," Cassidy said. "He has a key to this place, and he should be here any time now."

"Let's go," Dez said.

They took off toward the lighthouse. As soon as they got there, Austin pulled up. He unlocked the door, and they flooded inside.

"Let me," Dez said.

"Dez..."

"Please." Cassidy was more than capable, but Dez . . . he had personal reasons for wanting to protect Bree.

Cassidy frowned and nodded. "Go. I'll be right behind you."

They rushed up the stairs, and Dez prayed he wasn't too late.

BREE DESPERATELY DIDN'T WANT everything to end with Jill killing her atop the lighthouse in a fit of rage and bitterness. She prayed that wouldn't be the case. But fear claimed her body. Her thoughts. Maybe even her hope.

"I've thought about this a lot." Jill's eyes looked glassy and cold as she addressed Bree. "About how the best way to kill you would be. At first, when I sent you those threats, I was just blowing off steam. But the more I think about it, the more I think that it could be fun to let you go out with a bang."

Despite the wind around her, a thin layer of sweat formed across Bree's face.

Jill put the remote back into her pocket and pulled out her phone instead. As she did, she set the gun on the metal walkway, just out of Bree's reach.

"Since you're so much into getting attention, I thought that maybe I could catch all of this on camera." Jill flashed a smile. "Maybe we could even do a VideoStream live on all of this as it happens. What do you think?"

"I think that's a bad idea," Bree said. "But I have a feeling I can't talk you out of it, can I?"

"No, you can't." She hit a few buttons on her phone and then held it up to record. "This is Jill, and I'm here to talk about the rise and fall of Bree Jordan. You may think of her as the sweet girl next door with the voice of an angel. She is everything that I can't stand, and I want you all to be witnesses to what is going to happen to her. Say hi for the camera, Bree."

Bree only stared, determined not to play this woman's game. "You're sick, Jill."

"What she says about me really doesn't matter.

Because my mind is already made up. This will be the last day that Bree Jordan walks here on earth."

Bree sucked in a breath but tried not to show too much fear for the camera. That's what Jill wanted. Bree couldn't give her the satisfaction.

"Okay, maybe since you didn't say hi, you can say bye." Jill grabbed her gun and pointed it toward Bree.

Bree couldn't take her eyes off that barrel. One pull of the trigger, and she would be a goner. She wasn't ready for that yet.

Please, God. Send help. Don't let anyone else get hurt.

"Tell your audience that you're better than everybody else," Jill demanded.

"Why would I do that? It's *not* what I think."

"It's how you act," Jill snapped.

"I don't know about that. But I do know that's not who I am."

Jill didn't seem to hear her. "Sing the first verse of 'You're Killing Me.'"

"What? Now?" Had this woman lost her mind?

"That's right. Now." Jill pointed the gun, her finger on the trigger.

The message was clear: sing or else.

Bree scrambled to remember the lyrics. Finally, her voice squeaked as she began with, "I'm standing on the edge. Death is waiting for me. Death has your name. Death is all I see."

Jill smiled and raised her eyebrows. "Perfect. Climb to the other side of the railing."

"You want me to . . ." Bree looked below her and felt her head spin at the sheer height. "Jill . . . I'm not going to act out my song."

"I said do it!"

Bree heard the tone and knew this was no time to argue. Jill would pull the trigger.

Should she take her chances that she might be able to buy time until Dez could help her?

Neither option seemed tempting.

But she had to see if she could draw this out.

"Now!" Jill shouted.

"Okay! Okay!" Bree's hands trembled as she threw her leg over the railing. Carefully, she lowered herself to the other side. With one hand still cuffed, she gripped the metal with all her might, praying her feet didn't slip.

As she looked at the ground below, her head swam.

Please, Lord . . .

"On the count of three, you're going to sing your song while I record you. If you don't, I'm going to pull this trigger. Understand?"

Bree nodded. "I do."

The wind swept around her, nearly pushing her from her spot. She couldn't let this be the end. She had too much of life left to live.

Jill turned on her camera phone again and began recording herself. "Everyone, this is your chance to lift your prayers—as if they're going to do any good. Now, sing, Bree. Sing."

Bree opened her mouth but nothing came out.

"I can't hear you!"

"Don't you know that you're killing me . . ." Bree's voice cracked.

"This isn't nearly as fulfilling as I thought it would be," Jill muttered. "On second thought, I'll do this the easy way. I'm going to give you to the count of three. Then I'm pulling the trigger."

Ice filled her veins. "Don't do this, Jill," Bree said. "It's not too late."

"Yes, it is." Jill flashed a smile. "Three. Two."

CHAPTER THIRTY-SIX

DEZ HEARD everything that was being said. As far as he knew, Jill had no idea he and Cassidy lingered on the stairway. He had to make a move, and he had to make it soon.

Sirens sounded in the background. Help was on the way.

But they had no time to waste.

Dez heard Jill say, "Three, two—"

Before she could say "one," Dez reached out from the hatch and grabbed Jill's leg. He jerked it until the woman hit the platform with a thud. The gun dropped from her hand, along with her phone.

He knew he didn't have long. He had to make a move, and it had to be now.

Dez pulled himself from the hatch and straddled Jill. As he did, her hand reached out for her gun.

He couldn't let her reach it.

Cassidy scrambled past him toward Bree.

Jill's knees jammed into his back.

That wasn't going to stop him. He grabbed her wrists and flipped her over until her face was against the metal grate.

"This is all over," Dez told her. "Your little game is done."

Dez's gaze lifted to Bree. Just as Cassidy reached her, Bree lost her grip.

And she fell from the lighthouse.

BREE FELT herself slip and gasped. All of this, and she was still going to die, wasn't she?

Then a terrible pain ripped through her.

She was still holding on. Only her feet had slipped.

They dangled below her now.

Agony continued to tear through her arms from the impact of her body lurching to a stop.

She could already feel her grip loosening, her strength waning.

Cassidy appeared from above and grabbed her arms. "I've got you, Bree."

"Cassidy, Jill's all yours," Dez said. "I'll get Bree."

"I'm on it."

They traded places. Dez reached down and easily pulled Bree up and over the railing. As he gathered her in his arms, Cassidy passed him a key, and Dez unlocked the handcuff.

"Are you okay?"

Bree nodded, relief washing through her. She'd thought she was going to die. She'd been nearly certain of it. Who would have thought this handcuff could have saved her?

Dez gently touched her wrist. "I think it might be broken."

She squeezed the tears back from her eyes. She'd never felt pain like she did now, but gratitude won. She was alive. "But it will heal. Thank you. For everything."

He leaned down until their foreheads touched. His hands splayed across her neck and into her hair.

"I was so worried about you, Bree." His voice sounded raspy with emotion and concern. "Never do that again."

"If I thought it would protect you, I'd do it all over again."

He raised an eyebrow. "You really are stubborn sometimes, aren't you?"

She let out a whimpering laugh as she held her wrist. "Yes, I suppose that I am."

Wasting no more time, Dez closed the space between them until his lips met hers briefly.

Maybe everything would be okay. Finally.

CHAPTER THIRTY-SEVEN

THE NEXT DAY, Bree had a cast on her arm. Her wrist was broken, but the doctor said she'd be okay. Since the break was on her right arm and the cast didn't cover her elbow, she'd still be able to play the guitar. It would just require a little more creativity.

The whole confrontation between her and Jill had been caught on video. VideoStream removed it from its site, but not before some people had managed to copy the footage and distribute it to various media outlets. All the news stations wanted to play it over and over again.

And Bree's album sales had soared because of it.

Emerson had been formally charged with money laundering and conspiracy, among other things.

Bree's lawyer had filed a civil suit against him. Soon, her contract would be null and void.

That was okay with Bree, because other labels were trying to court her in the wake of everything that had happened.

Lloyd had survived the gunshot wound. He'd had nothing to do with this.

Trixie had been found. She was also okay. She'd even mumbled an apology to Bree when their paths had crossed at the clinic.

As her way of saying thank you, Bree would be doing a free concert here in Lantern Beach next month.

Right now, Bree was slated to do a press conference. This time, she decided to do it live. The guys from Blackout would be joining her.

"Are you ready for this?" Dez asked. They stood inside the police station. The press conference would take place outside in five minutes.

She nodded. "Yes, as a matter of fact, I am. I'm just happy right now to be alive."

"I'm happy that you're alive too." He scooted closer and kissed her forehead.

She couldn't believe just how easy things felt between the two of them. She'd feared that he was a player, that he would lose interest. And, granted, the relationship was still new, still fresh. But something in her gut told her that she could trust Dez.

"Let's do this," she said.

She stepped outside where microphones had been set up around a podium. Already, dozens of reporters were present, along with numerous fans. Thankfully, Bree had been in front of people enough to know how to handle herself.

Mayor MacArthur introduced her. Chief Chambers had defaulted to the man, insisting she was camera shy. Afterward, Bree gave a brief statement on what had happened. But it was what she had to say at the end that she was most excited about.

"Sometimes, I think we have it all messed up in our society. I am just a girl who can sing and entertain people, and I am hailed as a hero. I make entirely more money than I deserve. Meanwhile, there are men and women who put their lives on the line to fight for our country. They're sadly underpaid, and they don't get nearly the respect and attention that they deserve. I'm not the one who needs to be applauded or who needs to be on camera right now. But it's these people who are behind me who deserve all of the applause—former members of the US military."

Bree stepped back and clapped her hands. All around her, the crowd joined in.

She smiled, loving that she could use this moment for good.

When she'd first arrived here in Lantern Beach, she'd asked herself: is this all there is?

Now she knew the answer was no. There was so much more to life. She just had to seek it out.

DEZ HEARD what Bree was saying, and his admiration for her only grew. Bree could have easily made this day about herself, and instead she had chosen to give attention to the military. He had to respect that.

As everyone applauded, Dez looked at Bree and winked. She rewarded him with a huge smile.

As the clapping died down, she stepped back up to the microphone.

She was nothing like Leah, Dez realized. He'd used that as an excuse for entirely too long. But he was so glad that the truth had become clear. He'd just needed to give love another chance.

He never thought he would feel this smitten with somebody. It was a word that his mom liked to use, but it felt appropriate for this situation. Bree had captured all his thoughts and filled his desires for the future in a way he'd never experienced before.

He wished he could fully enjoy this moment and revel in his new relationship. But his visit with Brian Starks still hung over his head. Brian was still in a coma at a hospital in Raleigh. However, none of the Blackout team had forgotten his words.

They needed to decide their next step before there were more casualties in this unseen war.

Maybe he would think about that tomorrow. For now, he just wanted to enjoy this moment.

"Just one more thing until I take your questions," Bree said. "As a result of everything that has happened, there have been donations pouring in. Some of those have been coming in for the victims of the shooting here in Lantern Beach. Other donations have been pouring into the new nonprofit that I have set up."

New nonprofit? What was Bree talking about?

"I'm still in the process of getting all the paperwork signed, but, until then, I was able to set up an account online that will be overseen by a third party. The fund will be for people who are out of the military and who need help, so they can get what they need. All the donations that you make will be going to organizations like Hope House here in Lantern

Beach, North Carolina. It was started by a former Navy SEAL, and the organization works to help people adjust to civilian life after serving in the military."

Pride swelled in Dez's heart. If he had his way, he would never let Bree go.

EPILOGUE

AS SKYE STARTED down the aisle between the white foldout chairs set up on the beach, Bree began to play a new song that she'd written. She'd sung it for Skye earlier, and the bride-to-be loved it. She'd told Bree this was the one that she wanted played at her wedding.

Bree had thought she might think that.

The event was small and cozy but wonderful. The sun set behind the happy couple, smearing beautiful colors across the sky. The day was temperate, and the weather couldn't be any better. A small archway had been set up on the beach where Skye and Austin would say their vows to each other in a few minutes.

The event was casual, with no one really

dressing up. It was more beach casual with khaki pants and white linen shirts. Skye wore a beautiful vintage white gown that fit her Bohemian style.

There were probably only fifty people at the ceremony, but these were all the people closest to Skye and Austin. Briar, Skye's nine-year-old son, stood up for them as ringbearer.

The sight brought tears to Bree's eyes. It was truly beautiful.

Dez sat in the third row. As his eyes met hers, he winked again. Bree loved that the wink seemed to be reserved just for her.

She cleared her throat, knowing it was time for her to sing. Dez had yet to hear her new song. She wanted it to be a surprise for him also.

"You're my safe harbor,
The right kind of partner
To get me through the storms of life.
You're like an anchor,
And I want to say thank you
For keeping me grounded in the midst of strife.
Sheltered. Protected.
You're everything I never knew I was longing for
Right in front of me.
You've opened my eyes to what I really need.
You're my safe harbor."

When the wedding was over and the reception on the beach began, Dez pulled Bree toward him, and they swayed in each other's arms on a wooden platform that had been placed on the sand. String lights hung overhead, and the crashing of the waves soothed Bree's soul like only nature could. The night was perfect.

"That song was really beautiful," Dez murmured in her ear.

"You inspired it. Just like I said."

"Whoever thought that I could inspire a song. Can you tell my mama that? She'll put it on her wall of Dez."

"Her wall of Dez?"

He shrugged. "Yeah, you know—the one with all my school pictures, awards, trophies."

She chuckled. "I'm sure she's proud of you. But I bet you've inspired people way more than you ever even realized."

"You're going to make me blush, Bree Jordan. Or trip. Or spill something—things I never did until I met you."

She chuckled again. "I think it's adorable."

"I've always wanted to be adorable."

Her smile faded. "There's one more thing I wanted to tell you."

His smile faded. "What's that?"

"I've decided to stay on Lantern Beach for a couple more months. There's a lot that I need to figure out, and I had planned on taking a little break anyway. The new label I'm talking to wants me to do some of my own stuff, so I figured I would take some time to write some songs and have some downtime."

"That's great news."

"A private accounting firm has looked at Emerson's books. He owes a lot of people a lot of money. The good news is that he has cash in his accounts. Because of that, I should have a decent-sized check coming in. I would like to donate some of it to Blackout."

"What do you mean?" He twisted his head.

"I mean, I know that you guys are looking for a place to set up a permanent base. I don't know exactly what you're thinking or where or any of the details, but that's okay. When I finally get the payout that's coming to me, I'd like to donate money to you guys to help you out."

"You don't have to do that, Bree."

"You guys saved my life. It's the least I can do."

He lowered his voice. "Thank you. I'm sure the guys would really appreciate that."

"And one final thing," she added as they

continued to sway. "Guess who called me this morning?"

"Who?"

"One of my sisters. She's actually away at college, and she's been watching all of this unfold on the news. She said she was at my parents' house one night watching the news when this story came on and that mom got all teary-eyed."

"Your parents still love you."

"Maybe there is hope. Either way, my sister would like to come here to visit me."

"That's great. But will it get her in trouble with your parents?"

"She doesn't know, and she's okay with whatever the outcome is. She said she's ready to make her own decisions. I don't want to cause a rift between her and Mom and Dad, but I would love to see her."

"Maybe this is the start of restoration."

"I hope so. I really hope so. Because I'm ready for a new start."

Dez leaned closer. "So am I."

He began singing Bree's new song in her ear, his soothing tones filling her with delight.

She never wanted this moment to end.

DOING THE RIGHT THING WAS HIS HARDEST TASK YET

Griff McIntyre never expected his ex-wife,

Bethany, and three-year-old daughter, Ada, to show up on his doorstep. After someone tried to abduct Ada, Bethany is desperate to find safety. Now Griff's not letting either of them out of his sight.

DESPERATION BINDS THEM

Bethany knows Griff is the only one who can protect them, despite the fact that he broke her heart. But she'll do anything to protect her daughter —even if it means playing nicely with Griff. Maybe in the process she'll learn why he really left.

A SHOCKING SECRET THREATENS EVERYTHING

As danger ripples through their lives, Griff and Bethany must work together to protect their daughter. But an unseen enemy wants something from them . . . and will stop at nothing to get it. When disaster strikes, can Griff keep his family safe? Or will past mistakes bring the ultimate failure?

Order your copy HERE.

ALSO BY CHRISTY BARRITT:

Hidden Currents
Flood Watch
Storm Surge
Dangerous Waters
Perilous Riptide
Deadly Undertow

LANTERN BEACH PD

When Cassidy Chambers accepted the job as police chief on Lantern Beach, she knew the island had its secrets. But a mysterious group that's moved onto the island will test all her skills. Cassidy enlists the help of her husband, former Navy SEAL Ty Chambers. Not everything is as it seems, and, as facts materialize, danger on the island grows. Can Cassidy and Ty discover the truth about the shadowy crimes in their cozy community? Or has darkness permanently invaded their beloved Lantern Beach?

On the Lookout
Attempt to Locate
First Degree Murder
Dead on Arrival
Plan of Action

THE WORST DETECTIVE EVER:

I'm not really a private detective. I just play one on TV.

Joey Darling, better known to the world as Raven Remington, detective extraordinaire, is trying to separate herself from her invincible alter ego. She played the spunky character for five years on the hit TV show *Relentless*, which catapulted her to fame and into the role of Hollywood's sweetheart. When her marriage falls apart, her finances dwindle to nothing, and her father disappears, Joey finds herself on the Outer Banks of North Carolina, trying to piece together her life away from the limelight. But as people continually mistake her for the character she played on TV, she's tasked with solving real life crimes . . . even though she's terrible at it.

USA Today has called Christy Barritt's books "scary, funny, passionate, and quirky."

Christy writes both mystery and romantic suspense novels that are clean with underlying messages of faith. Her books have won the Daphne du Maurier Award for Excellence in Suspense and Mystery, have been twice nominated for the Romantic Times Reviewers' Choice Award, and have finaled for both a Carol Award and Foreword Magazine's Book of the Year.

She is married to her Prince Charming, a man who thinks she's hilarious—but only when she's not trying to be. Christy is a self-proclaimed klutz, an avid music lover who's known for spontaneously bursting into song, and a road trip aficionado.

When she's not working or spending time with her family, she enjoys singing, playing the guitar, and exploring small, unsuspecting towns where people have no idea how accident-prone she is.

Find Christy online at:
www.christybarritt.com
www.facebook.com/christybarritt
www.twitter.com/cbarritt

Sign up for Christy's newsletter to get information on all of her latest releases here: www. christybarritt.com/newsletter-sign-up/

If you enjoyed this book, please consider leaving a review.